The Beanie INVASION

"Unofficial"

Janie Daniels
(BEANIEOLOGIST)

Best Wishes

Janie E. Daniels

This book contains valuable information:

Short stories, articles, surveys and Interviews which are all based on the world famous Ty's Beanie Babies®.

This book was designed to be read by individuals aged 10 and up.

Acknowledgments

Many thanks to:
My family: Mike, Jennifer and David,
for their support and encouragement;
Mr. Randy Jones for believing in me and
encouraging me to write.

Dedication

This book is dedicated to
Mr. Randy Jones
of
The Beanie Babies Buddies Club
and all of the Beanie collectors in the world.

ESPECIALLY THE KIDS!

THE FUTURE BELONGS TO THE CHILDREN.
THEY ARE FULL OF
HOPE,
DREAMS,
AND IMAGINATION.

Janie Daniels

CONTENTS

CHAPTER ONE

My Story and How
Beanies Invaded My Life

Up until December 1996 I had never heard of Beanie Babies. When I first spotted Beanies my initial reaction was that they were cute. Then I remembered my children really didn't need any more stuffed animals. I continued to shop, but for some reason I kept being drawn back to Beanies like a magnet. After first resisting, I finally gave in and decided that they would make excellent stocking-stuffers for Christmas. I had no idea at the time that making the initial purchase would cause these little adorable stuffed animals to consume so much of my life from that point forward.

On Christmas morning the children peered around the corner, eyed their stockings and discovered their Beanies. They screamed with joy!

My husband hooked the family up to the Internet as a Christmas present. (I had purchased my computer six months ago and had just gotten over the fear of turning it on.) The thought of the Internet was overwhelming for me, but on the other hand the thought of traveling the world without having to leave my home excited me. In late January I finally got up my nerve to start surfing the Internet. I really did not have anything I wanted to see, so I typed in "Beanie Babies" into my search engine. Much to my surprise there were over 13,000 different locations for me to search. I found myself spending hours reading through all of the web sites, as well as the Ty home page (www.ty.com, #1 site for Beanie Babies).

As I read this site, I learned that they had just retired a few of their Beanies in January. This meant that these retired Beanies would now become more valuable. I knew I had to act quickly to locate these little critters before anyone else did, or I simply would be out of luck. I called my sister-in-law to see if my niece was interested in collecting the set. She told me that she had already gone through that phase. About a week later she called back and said that they had changed their minds, they did want to collect Beanie Babies. I then filled her in on what was happening in the Beanie world. I explained about how Ty had just retired a few of their Beanies and told her we would have to move fast. I had bookmarked a couple of Beanie Babie web sites. Magan's site had a store directory in it. I started calling all of the numbers listed. After several hours and an enormous phone bill, I was able to locate all of the newly-retired Beanies. I had paid as little as $5 for most, $25 for a few and $30 for Tabasco, my highest priced one.

During the next couple of weeks I was glued to my computer and the Internet; they had become my best friends. "I was hooked"! I spent anywhere from six to eight hours a day reading every site that contained Beanie information. When I was not on the Internet, I was on the phone contacting family and friends asking for help. I found myself quizzing other mothers at school if they knew what Beanies were. My best friend, Sue, and her daughter had been collecting them for some time. They shared information with me that helped me to obtain quite a few that we needed. Sue then decided that since I had made the decision to collect the whole set, she would give me Ashley's list to complete. Before long my purse was filled with Beanie wish-lists, and I was determined to find all that were needed!

Every morning after getting the children ready for school, I would spend my time calling various stores looking for Beanies. I remember the first time I went into a store that had "tons" of them on shelves. I could feel my blood pressure rising. I was so excited that I starting grabbing them by the handful. When I finally came out of my delirium and realized what I was doing, I took a deep breath, quickly grabbed the lists out of my purse, then calmly started checking off the ones they had. I remember driving home that day thinking to myself, "How had I gotten so wrapped up in this?" I even wondered if these toys had some sort of scent that attracted people into buying them. I had never acted this way about a toy before.

Day after day I found myself falling into the same routine. One morning I woke up early to do some house cleaning before I ventured out looking for Beanies. I was scrubbing down my bathroom, as I was hurrying I accidentally hit my head on the toilet paper rack that had no toilet paper in it. I hit it so hard that I literally knocked the rack off the wall. As I sat on the floor realizing how much it hurt, I noticed that I was bleeding. The first thought that came to my mind was panic. The second thought was "Oh no, this cannot be happening!" A store was due for a large shipment today, and I had to be there to collect my Beanies. I called my husband at work and explained what had happened. I also called my friend Sue thinking that I might need stitches, and she would have to stay with the children. They both arrived at approximately the same time. They found my daughter, Jennifer, consoling me and applying pressure to the area. They explained to me how head wounds tend to bleed a lot, and that the cut was only big enough for maybe one or two stitches. They advised me to lie low because they anticipated my having an enormous headache. After they left I took a few Advil and decided to work with the Internet again. After a few hours I decided that I had to venture out and look for my Beanies. There was no way that I was going to disappoint my children when they returned home from school asking what I had found. I had already decided that they would have to earn the Beanies by making good grades and by doing chores around the house. There was no way this mom was going to work this hard and just turn over the goodies for nothing. I also knew that I had to have a good supply on hand for rewards!

CHAPTER TWO

How I Met the Beanie Master

During my Internet search for Beanies I ran across a club called the Beanie Babies Buddies Club. I had been thinking for some time about joining this club. It had a lot to offer, and I liked the fact that it was not a commercial site just offering to sell items. It also had a members' table where you could e-mail large groups of people at one time about anything you wanted. (Preferably about Beanies!)

I remember the day I e-mailed the Beanie Master about wanting to join his club. Immediately I received his reply welcoming me into the club. The next day my name appeared on the members' table. I recalled seeing the option to say "hi" to other Beanie lovers by using the members' table. I typed a short message offering for adults to relate to me their Beanie stories. The next day, when I accessed my e-mail I had over 30 responses to my request. Before I knew it, I was talking to people all over the world and loving it. After about a week, I decided that I wanted to access the members' table again. This time I put out a notice about my being an old-fashion mom with traditional values, and I needed their help. I asked if people would mind sending me copies of newspaper articles so that I might include them in a scrap book that I was preparing for my children. Once again I received several replies, some offering to share, and others requesting copies of articles for their own scrap books. One message I received came from the Beanie Master. I remember thinking to myself that I must be getting a warning about using the members' table in this manner; but instead, he was offering to send me a copy from his own local paper. I was impressed, he would not allow me to send a self-addressed stamped envelope for the article. Little did I know at that time that this would be the start of something new.

I found myself using the members' table to get Beanie information out to club members on a regular basis. The next message I sent regarded a situation I witnessed at a local store.

Hello Fellow Club Members,
Here's wishing you all a very Happy Easter and a delightful Spring.
Now, let's get to the latest Beanie Babie news:
Last week I sent a notice in reference to Ty's New Policy. It explained how the Ty company would be limiting the number of shipments of Beanie Babies to each store. The message also contained information about Maple, the Canadian Bear.
I have a little story I would like to share with you.
Yesterday I went to the store looking for Beanie Babies for Easter. I arrived at approximately 1:15. There were people everywhere, but I didn't see any Beanie Babies. I talked to a few people to find out when they would arrive.
The Manager of the store announced over the loud speaker for everyone to please leave the store and come back around 3 o'clock. Many people refused to

leave, and instead got angry and accused the store of hiding the Beanie Babies in the back room. At this point I decided to leave and try to come back later.

I tried to return to the store around 3 o'clock and could not get into the parking lot. I went home and called the store to see if they had any left. The clerk who answered the phone was very upset and sounded as though she had been crying. I explained that I had been in the store earlier, but left at the managers' request. She said the matter had gone from bad to worse. She added the police had been called in for crowd control because of flaring tempers.

The point that I'm trying to make is this:

Now that the Ty company's policy of April 1, 1997, is in effect, we can expect more of this to happen. The shops that do not sell Ty's plush line, will have to in order to be able to get Beanie Babies. Ty's plush line contained a variety of other stuffed animals, but was also more costly. The problem is a lot of store can't afford to sell the plush line.

The next time you buy a Beanie Baby think about how lucky you are that you even found them. Remind people not to be rude to the sales clerks. Sales clerks are there to do a job, not be brought to tears by customers screaming for Beanie Babies.

I never realized the Beanie Master was keeping an eye on me. One day I got a message from him asking me if I would be interested in writing articles for his site. I responded that I would consider it and sent him a copy of a letter I had written to Ty. The next day I got another note from the Beanie Master asking me to click on the site outlined in blue. I went to the site and, much to my surprise, saw that he had created a page entitled "Latest News From Ms. Janie's Beanie Babie Central." I sent him a message indicating that I felt he obviously was not going to take "no" for an answer. He replied that this page could only be viewed by the two of us and he only wanted to show me a sample.

A couple of long days went by and I could not get his offer off my mind. I have always enjoyed writing since I was a child, and could not help but think that this might be the opportunity I was looking for. And, if nothing else, I knew it could be fun. I contacted the Beanie Master and told him that I had decided to take him up on his offer. We e-mailed each other every other day just making small talk and getting used to one another.

The Big Day had finally come! I had figured out how to write my first story which was to be posted on the Beanie Babies Buddies Club site. McDonald's was introducing Teenie Beanies in their "Happy Meal," and today was the first day of the introduction. I had to get the story!!!

Once the story was posted, I started receiving e-mail from across the county. People would ask me where I had found my Beanie Babies, and if I could help them find them as well. I even had a lady ask me about the area I lived in. She was military and was getting ready to move to my area and wanted some information. The amount of e-mail I was generating was not only overwhelming it was beginning to get scary! I had people really needing my help. I had to make sure I was factual and quick to respond.

Soon after I got started writing articles, I was contacted by my local newspaper requesting an interview. I spent three days preparing for it. Every picture I had ever seen taken of Beanie Babies had been taken with them piled up in front of the person. I wanted to do something different so I asked my friends, Sue and Sarah, if they would help me decorate my office with Beanies. We had approximately three hundred Beanie Babies all over my office. We made posters and arranged the Beanies according to retired ones, current ones, and the original nine.

When the morning came for the interview, the photographer wanted me to dump all of the Beanies on the floor and for me to stand or kneel behind them. I explained how I thought that this picture should be different from all of the others. He went along with me and took several pictures. Then the reporter showed up to do the interview. At first I felt very uncomfortable as I wasn't sure what to expect. After a few questions, the more comfortable I became. Before long he could not get a word in edge-wise. I showed him my book-marks and the stack of e-mail I had received. I took him into my two favorite sites, "The Beanie Babies Club" and "Magan's Beanie Babies." The interview lasted a little over an hour.

After a week passed without seeing the interview in the paper, I contacted the reporter and asked when should I expect to see it. He stated that the article had become so long that it might take another week. On April 16, 1997 the interview finally came out. The reporter, Mr. Beau Yarbrough of the "Potomac News," had done a fine job. The article took up well over three quarters of the front page of the "Lifestyles" section and carried over on to another page.

The article benefited me in so many ways it was unbelievable! I was hearing from people I have not heard from in a few years. The children at school were calling me the "Beanie Lady." My kids felt special to think that their mom was getting so much attention, which in turn also drew attention to them. After Mr. Yarbrough informed me that the Associated Press had picked up the article to be offered in many states, I then received a phone call from the Associated Press wire services asking if they could conduct a phone interview. The situation had become so overwhelming, that sometimes I didn't sleep more than four hours a night! I thought that this alone should qualify me as a certified "Beanieoligist!"

✑   ✑   ✑   ✑   ✑

Once the article was published in other areas, many strange occurrences started to happen. My husband was paid a visit by a friend of his who was in our wedding nineteen years ago. It had been some time since the two of them had spoken. He told my husband that he was reading his local paper and the article on the front page caught his attention. It was my Beanie article. He said he recognized my picture and it made him think about the "good old days," so he thought he would pay a visit. I also got a phone call from Mr. Yarbrough, asking me if I would call one of the viewers of the article. He explained how he did not want to give out my phone number or e-mail address without my permission and informed me that a woman had contacted him at the paper attempting to reach me. He gave me the women's phone number and also expressed how excited he was about the Associated Press picking up the story from the wires. He said that this was a first for him, and it was a pretty big deal in the newspaper business.

I placed the phone call to the woman who had contacted the paper. She explained that she was trying to find Beanie Babies for her grandchildren and asked if I sold Beanies or if I knew of any place where she could find them. We talked for a while, then I gave her my address and asked her to keep in touch. A few days later I received a note from her thanking me for calling and enclosed was a $1 bill for the phone call.

This article kept my e-mail jumping. I found myself spending hours just answering messages. Most of the questions I was able to answer fairly easily, but some required my doing some research. I began answering my home phone as "Beanie Babie Central." This made a lot of people laugh.

My son, David Daniels, in my Beanie Babie Central Office

My daughter, Jennifer Daniels, at Beanie Babie Central.

CHAPTER THREE

McDonalds and Teenie Beanies— Four Stories

McDonalds and Ty had struck a deal! The whole world was waiting for the arrival of these miniature versions of Beanie Babies. There was much anticipation as well as speculation. Many eager kids and adults lined up at McDonalds to be able to claim the right of owning their own Teenie Beanies.

These next four stories will guide you through this much published event from start to finish.

Latest News from Janie's Beanie Central

Today is April 11th and we all know what that means…
THE TEENIE BEANIES HAVE ARRIVED!

My morning began with strategy planning. How was I going to get this story? How many Happy Meals was I going to have to eat? Was I going to be able to get through the crowds of people? I thought to myself, I'd better wear my tennis shoes, it was going to be a long day. I called a local McDonalds located in Dale City, Va. and spoke with the store supervisor, Wanda Blevins. I told Mrs. Blevins that I would like to do a story on the Teenie Beanies. She agreed to meet with me and allowed me to take pictures.

Arriving at the store at 9:15 and imagine my surprise at finding people already waiting for the Happy Meals to go on sale at 11:00 AM! Mrs. Blevins was extremely courteous and answered the following questions:

Janie—How many Beanie Babies did you get in?
Mrs. Blevins—Eight cases with 150 per case.
Janie—Are you ready for the crowds today?
Mrs. Blevins—Yes, we have put extra people on staff, it's a good thing school was out because I was able to get more people to work. We will have the Happy Meal bags ready with toys in them, all we will have to do is add the food.
Janie—Will you be glad when this is over?
Mrs. Blevins—Yes, I don't understand why they are so popular, but I must admit that they are cute.
Janie—Which Beanie Babie is your favorite?
Mrs. Blevins—Patti, I like the colors. (Patti is a Platypus)
Janie—Do you expect more than the original eight cases you got in?
Mrs. Blevins—We are trying to get more, we may have to buy them from other stores, I just don't know right now.
Janie—When you sell out of the first two cases you have, will you start selling the next week's supply?
Mrs. Blevins—Yes, the two for next week are Chops the lamb and Chocolate the moose.

I also spoke with the store manager, Heidi:

Janie—Heidi, would you like to comment on this Beanie Babie craze?
Heidi—It's wild, I'll be glad when it's over.

Janie—Which one is your favorite?
Heidi—Patti, the platypus.

During this interview I also learned that this McDonalds has Happy Meals for 99 cents on Tuesday, Wednesday and Thursday. (This price includes the Teenie Beanies.) On Thursday nights they offer a craft directed by Doris Zuengs and Ginny, McDonalds employees. They offer such crafts as seed charts, clocks, butterfly making and more. Best of all, the crafts are free. I truly believe that this McDonalds knows how to put a smile on a kid's face.

Their store policy is a free Teenie Beanie with each Happy Meal purchase. Thanks to Wanda, and Doris for allowing me to do this interview. They are truly good Samaritans.

> **UPDATE:** I spoke with Wanda Blevins around 2 PM. She sounded exhausted. She said they had sold out of this week's products and had already started on next week's shipment. Wanda is allowing me to follow this story 'til the end, so look for more updates to come.

Latest News from Janie's Beanie Central

During the course of investigating the McDonalds Teenie Beanies I found that the company-owned stores did not want to be interviewed. I went into one McDonalds to speak with a Manager or Supervisor, but neither were available. I then proceeded to take pictures of the lines of people waiting to collect their Happy Meals with their Teenie Beanies. One of the store's employees asked me not to take pictures, saying they were not allowed. I replied "Don't you have birthday parties here? I know people take pictures at those types of parties, I've done it myself." No reply; they just didn't want to talk. I packed up my camera and my writing materials and left. I then visited the McDonalds at Prince William

Commons. I spoke with the manager, Rolando Castaneda. He was very pleasant and took the time to answer a few questions:

Janie—How has the Teenie Beanies affected business?
Rolando—Very good, more people are coming in than
    before.
Janie—Which one of the Teenie Beanies is your favorite?
Rolando—I like Chops the Lamb.
Janie—Will you be glad to see this all end?
Rolando—I will be glad somewhat; but, I also will be sad
    because I know business will slow down again.
Janie—How many cases of Teenie Beanies did you receive?
Rolando—Eight cases with 150 per case. Composed of
    three different styles.
Janie—Were you prepared for the overwhelming crowds?
Rolando—I did put extra people on today, but I really
    didn't expect the crowds to be as bad as they were.
*Janie—Have you gotten lots of calls about your Teenie
    Beanies?*
Rolando—Yes, a lot!

As I was sitting in this McDonalds eating my Happy Meal with my children, I could hear grandmothers exchanging information on where to get Beanie Babies in town, kids yelling, "Which one did you get?" and moms saying "Sit down and be quiet." As I watched one mom with five children bring the meals to the table, the kids swarmed around her like bees. She just handed them out one by one without even looking to see who got what. As soon as the bags were opened, the trading began. The mom even traded her Patti for Chops.

I decided to go over and speak to this family. I introduced myself and inquired whether I could ask a couple of questions. I learned that the family lived in Lake Ridge, VA and the mom's name was Dorothy. They had been expecting and looking forward to this day for a little over two weeks. I asked the children which ones were their favorites. They yelled: Quakers the duck, Pinky the flamingo, Speedy the turtle, Lizzy the lizard and Seamore the seal.

I would like to thank Mr. Castaneda for allowing me to interview him and for being so pleasant—especially during what was undoubtedly one of his busiest days of the year.

UPDATE: April 15th, McDonald's

I decided since Wanda had now sold Happy Meals with Teenie Beanies in them for the last five days, it was time to do an update:

Janie—How have things changed for you and your store since Happy Meals came out last Friday?

Wanda—I find myself dreaming about Beanie Babies. None of us at the store want to answer the phone; we know we will hear, "What Teenie Beanies do you have?"

Janie—Is this the hottest item McDonalds has ever put into their Happy Meals?

Wanda—Yes, "Hot can't touch it." It's too hot. I've been with McDonalds for 17 years and I have never seen anything like this before!!!

Janie—How many Happy Meals do you estimate selling since last Friday?

Wanda—Over 2,000.

Janie—Will you still be glad to see this all end?

Wanda—Yes, I can't wait.

Janie—Do you have any funny or unusual stories you would like to share?

Wanda—I think the funniest story is when I find business people coming in to buy Happy Meals just to get the Teenie Beanies; then they give the food away.

Janie—Do you happen to know if McDonalds and Ty will be working together again in the future?

Wanda—I don't know if they will.

Janie—*What is McDonalds going to do if they run out of the Teenie Beanies?*

Wanda—They are trying to make them as fast as they can, but when they are gone, they're gone.

Janie—*What is your sales for a normal lunch period, and how much has it increased since you started with this promotion?*

Wanda—We normally sell around $300 worth of food, now we are up to $700 for lunch alone.

Janie—*I don't understand why people can't come into your store and just purchase the Teenie Beanie for the price of a Happy Meal without having to buy food. Would you please explain this?*

Wanda—Because that is not the promotion. If someone doesn't want the food, it should be taken to a homeless shelter, church, daycare, or even the fire station.

Janie—*Are you collecting a set of the Teenie Beanies for yourself?*

Wanda—Yes, because it is a McDonalds toy and I collect them all.

Janie—*As part of the promotion there is supposed to be a case displaying the current 77 Beanie Babies. There is also supposed to be entry forms for the customer to fill out and possibly win the Beanies. Do you know why a lot of the stores are not doing this part of the promotion?*

Wanda—I would say that we do not display the case because we would be afraid of it being stolen. As far as the entry forms, that's up to each store owner. We try to help our customers as much as we can; we even send them to our other store locations that may have the Teenie Beanies they are looking for.

During this interview I learned that this McDonalds was out of Teenie Beanies until the next Thursday. On that

Thursday they expected to receive all ten of them. I also learned that, once again, this store had gone the extra mile in customer service. They had some customers that called and placed their food orders for $10 or more, and this McDonalds was willing to deliver. They went to places such as businesses and schools. That's what I call "Real Service with a Smile!"

I plan to visit Wanda and her store for one last update sometime in the next two weeks, or sooner if they sell out for good.

As Promised...The Final Interview with Wanda from McDonalds

Will this be the end of Teenie Beanies?

(While preparing for this last interview, a survey was taken about what questions the public would like for me to ask. These questions were asked of Beanie Babies Buddies Club members. http://www.netreach.net/~rjones/beanie.html as well as Magan's Beanie Babies. I'd like to thank both of these popular sites for allowing me to post my survey on the web site.)

The most popular question asked was: *Are there going to be more Teenie Beanies in the future?*

When Wanda was asked this question her reply was as follows:

> "I would not mind if McDonalds decided to promote these again, but they would have to be better prepared with a lot more items for us to sell. McDonalds had no idea how popular Beanie Babies would be. Half of us at the store didn't even know what they were."

I ask Wanda which ones were most popular and were hard to find:

"Pinky and Chocolate—They sold first and after that you couldn't find them anywhere."

How many phone calls a day did you receive about Teenie Beanies?

"It would be easier to explain it this way. Out of a 10 hour day we may get eight regular phone calls, but the phone never stopped ringing. In five minutes we would receive 30 to 40 different calls about the product. Every time you hung the phone up, it would ring!"

How many Teenie Beanies did you sell a day?

"Over 2,000."

At the beginning it was reported that the Teenie Beanies would probably not be worth much in the future. When I asked Wanda this question again, it had changed.

"Teenie Beanies will be worth a lot to McDonalds Collectors."

How long did it take you to completely deplete stock of Teenie Beanies?

"The promotion was suppose to last four weeks; we barely made it through one week. We received over 15 cases one week from the date that the promotion started and sold out in less than nine hours!!!"

I asked Wanda, in her opinion, who made the Teenie Beanies?

"Everything I have heard as a supervisor leads me to believe Ty made them."

Why didn't McDonalds stick with its originally stated game plan, and only sell two of the Teenie Beanies each week?

Wanda Blevins, McDonalds Supervisor

Wanda, Ronald, and Doris (Teenie Beanie Display Case)

David and Jennifer Daniels (My Little Angels)

"If we had done that, our customers would have been upset. They wanted to buy whatever we had until they were all gone. Customer service comes first. You have to please your customers."

Now that just about every kid in America has eaten Happy Meals until they are sick of them, what will you do in order to encourage them to keep coming back to McDonalds?

"Kids always want to come to McDonalds!! From now through May 22nd there is a special on Big Mac's, and starting on May 23rd there will be a special on Quarter Pounders with cheese. They will each cost 55 cents each; check your local McDonalds for details."

Some of the kids wanted to know why stitched eyes were on the Teenie Beanies instead of the plastic eyes?

"There was a safety issue involved, they had to be made safe for all ages."

One person wanted to know whether McDonalds had more than one secret sauce?

"All of our sauces are secret; you can not buy them any-where. They are all made exclusively by McDonalds."

For those of you who may be interested in the McDonalds Collectors Club, contact your local McDonalds Main Office for details.

I would like to thank all of you who participated in my survey and I would like once again to especially thank Wanda for allowing me to interview her.

CHAPTER FOUR

Elmtree Interview

This is an interview that was conducted on April 25, 1997 between Janie Daniels and Mr. Bob Martin. Bob and his partners Chuck & Jackie Leopold own seven Elmtree stores which sell Beanie Babies. I thought it would be nice to interview someone who would be able to answer some questions, and give me their views on Ty, Inc.

It was time to start writing more articles. I was starting to miss the excitement of not knowing how they would turn out or how the public viewed them. I wanted to know how store owners felt about Ty and their Beanie Babies. I had heard so much controversy about a love-hate relationship and that intrigued me to take my search to a higher level. I called one of my favorite stores and asked if they would contact the owner to see if he would grant me an interview. Mr. Bob Martin agreed and a time and place were scheduled.

I was very nervous about conducting this interview. After all, I was not a true reporter. I was just a woman who really enjoyed writing and wanted to keep collectors informed about information I had researched.

I met with Mr. Martin at one of his store locations and conducted the interview. After the first couple of questions, I could feel myself beginning to relax. Mr. Martin was not only very professional, he was also very candid. This interview was entitled "In Depth: Elmtree Beanie Babies and Ty."

The interview was posted at the Beanie Babies Buddies Club and became an instant hit. I was starting to receive e-mail messages from other establishments wanting me to interview them as well. Collectors were impressed with the article and how it could go from serious to humorous just by adding my own personal pictures. Kids loved the article because now they knew of another shop that would allow them to enter their name on a Beanie wish list.

Mr. Martin would you please give us a Bio on yourself?

"I was born in central Pennsylvania. I was in the Army for five and one-half years, I worked for the Defense Department until February 1995. I started this business in 1978 as a method of putting the youngsters through school. I have five children."

How did you first hear about Beanie Babies?

"Sales Rep. Ron Bauch with Mid Atlantic Sales, called up last summer around July or August, I told him I was not interested. In September a manager from Elden Street Market Place hit me with a two by four and woke me up. I called Bauch back and placed our initial order with him; it's been a go from there."

Were you glad to see Ty rescind the 10% policy?

"Yes Ma'am!"

How has this decision affected your store, and why were you glad to see it rescinded?

"I thought it was unethical. It would be the same as asking you if you bought a Beanie Babies here for $5.00 to buy at least 50 cents worth of another product. And that's not the way the retail market place works."

Now that Ty has canceled the required 10% plush are they giving stores any other incentives to buy the plush line? If so, what is the incentive?

"Nothing has been verbalized or sent to me in writing."

Have you ever regretted signing a contract with Ty?

"You don't sign a contract with Ty, they use purchase orders. There is no contractual relationship, that's probably my beef with Ty. They entered into contracts with certain large houses. During the first part of 1997 those contracts were fulfilled, but the orders for the small stores were not; we stood around waiting, but the big guns got their product."

So which stores are you talking about?

"Nordstroms, Cracker Barrel, and MJ Designs. They claimed it was a mistake but it was a corporate contract."

What do you think caused or started the Beanie craze?

"I really have no idea. They're not offensive, they don't take sides, they don't do anything, so it is left up to the imagination. Possibly the kids got into them because they found that they could play with them and use their imagination. Boys can be boys and girls can be girls and there is nothing offensive about the Beanies."

As a store owner, do you think this is a passing fad or is Ty enticing the buyer by "retiring items and introducing new items?"

"If Ty was smart in the collectable business then it would do exactly that; they would introduce a new product, retire an older product and form a club called the Beanie Babies Club. It would offer a special inducement to the club member to belong to the club and allow them to buy certain pieces that they could not buy on the open market. It would basically control the distribution for the demand of the product."

How consistent is Ty? For example—they said they would not fill back orders, but they are still doing it? They also said their warehouses are empty, but somehow Beanies are still managing to show up.

"I would rather say that Ty has gotten itself caught up in a phenomenon that it didn't appreciate. They are trying to put out some standard polices; unfortunately, there are too many people involved. You might talk to Ty on Tuesday for an hour and be told that there is nothing in the warehouse, that June 1st will be the earliest delivery. Then have your manager call you and say Hallmark just received 5,000 Beanie Babies, Nordstroms just got 12,000. I think that's a problem of not being wise enough to understand what was going on."

Have you found that the quality of the Beanie Babies being made now is not up to Ty's normal quality standards?

"In the last two orders for February and April we had damage, which we never had in the original orders. One of our managers took the pieces home and hand stitched them. It's obvious that there is some rushing going on somewhere."

What guarantee do store owners have for receiving timely orders?

"They will endeavor to ship your April order in 30 days, that's it. But then again customer service says there is nothing in the warehouse till June 1st."

Did Ty mislead, misrepresent or otherwise understate their ability to deliver products or honor contracts?

"I don't think they misstated, there was just no guarantee, but they definitely under estimated."

What do you think about Beanie Babies going from a child's toy to a mother's hysteria?

"As a retailer you like the sales, but at the same time you sort of wonder where the priorities are. When you see the kids come in with an envelope of money that they saved looking to buy a Beanie Baby with, you sort of have some misgivings because you don't have it. You don't have it because the adults came in and bought them all."

How do you feel about Ty selling to Nordstroms?

"We talked to Ron Bauch twice, when he approached us the first time, and when we went back. Ron said it looks like we made a mistake. We apologized and said we would like to get the Beanie Babies and do business. Part of the verbal discussion was that the product was being managed in terms of its distribution. It would not be mass marketed and would not be in large department stores, it would be sold only to gift shops, floral shops, small retail shops, hospital gift shops and card shops, because it was designed for the youngster and this was a place a youngster could go. Some stores do not fit that description; I have a problem with them getting this product based on the verbal agreement."

How reliable is Ty's retired list? I understand items have been labeled retired, but up to four months later are still being made and shipped to stores. What can you tell me about this?

"We have not had much luxury in receiving retired pieces. We have put retired pieces on our order with our Sales Representative. This order was placed before the retirement was announced, and in some cases we would get a few pieces."

Do Ty's purchase orders stay the same? Or do they change regularly?

"With the 10% they were going to come out with a two-part order form, since they receded that the orders that we did on April 3rd with Mid Atlantic were the same old order sheets. All we can order is 36 of any one piece, as my credit limit, restricts the total number of orders per month."

Do you plan to continue selling Beanie Babies?

"As long as the free market place process continues. I really don't want to get into crowd control problems.

Mary, kissing Legs the Frog. Manager at Potomac Mills Elmtree.

Elmtree manager Judy, Proudly displaying the teacher section of her store.

We have tried since this process started in December to build a relationship that is positive with the customer. It's also true that the handwriting for the request list has gone from young people's handwriting to adults' handwriting but, at the same time, if a customer comes into the store and makes a request, we will do our best to fill it. And once that's taken care of, the product will be put on the floor. We have been fairly pleased that the customers have restrained themselves. In fact, we have seen many instances of cooperation taking place. We hope it is because of the way we have dealt with the situation."

Are you going to limit the number per customer in the future?

"We have not placed a limit, but we have put basic guidelines for the managers. When a shipment comes in, pull your customers request first, then put the rest on the floor for sale. We are trying to be fair and we want to take care of our local customers."

Most of the stores in the area have either decided to quit taking lists for their customers, or seem irritated with the mention of Beanie Babies. Why do you still honor your customer request lists?

"We are a local gift shop, we want to build a relationship with our customers in the area. I don't know how we can claim to be a service orientated business and not try to provide some reasonable amount of level of accommodation."

Do you think the Beanie Babies fad will last much longer?

"If Ty does not get it's process under control, people will get tired of it and stop collecting them. Children's attention span is very short, and adults will give up if the process is too hard."

What special services do your stores give to your customers?

"We do not ship our Beanie Babie product. We keep them in our stores for our customers. 'Local only.'"

How many stores do you have in the area? What are their locations?

"Potomac Mills—Potomac Mills Mall 2700 Potomac Mills Circle—Manager Mary
Center Plaza—4319 Dale Blvd, Woodbridge, VA—Manager Judy
Lake Ridge Commons—12431 Hedges Run Drive, Lake Ridge, VA—Manager Linda
Manassas Junction—8827 Centerville Road, Manassas, VA—Manager Rebecca
Cardinal Forest Center—8322 B. Old Keene Mill Rd, Springfield, VA—Manager Annie
Elden Street Market—1230 Elden Street, Herndon, VA—Manager Roberta
Mapledale Plaza—5429 Mapledale Place, Dale City, VA—Manager Janice"

What other product lines do you offer at your stores?

"Precious Moments, Boyds Bears, very unique lines, each one of them has a character. Yankee Candles, best longer lasting scent of any candle we know. They also have an accessory line with baskets to put the candles in. We have also found that people have such little time these days that they grab and go. They are looking for help to provide leads to express themselves. We started gift bags and baskets, we provide ideas, customers go through the store collecting merchandise to put into the bags or baskets and we personalize them any way they want."

Do you offer your customers a discount or coupon as an incentive for shopping at your stores? Do you pass out customer appreciation cards?

"We try to offer the customer appreciation card to everybody, sometimes we do forget. If anyone does not have one, they can obtain one. This card has value, it can be deducted from any future purchase."

Is there anything you would like to add or tell your customers?

"I think a shopping experience should be a fun experience. We fully recognize people don't have enough time to shop the way they used to; we are open for suggestions in order to make their shopping experience a pleasant one."

After this interview. Bob and I walked around the store at Potomac Mills and I learned some pretty interesting things. The Yankee candles which Bob spoke about had a story behind them. He opened up a candle and ask me to smell it and identify it's aroma. I replied, "Men's aftershave." He then went on to tell me that college girls would buy this product called "Midsummer's Night" in a Yankee Candle, light it in their dorm rooms, and all the other girls would think that there was a man in the dorm. I also learned that today, after more than two decades of waving the "Gift of home fragrancing" banner, Yankee Candles are the most widely recognized specialty scented candles in the United States.

I also noticed a plush line called "Fiesta." I have to admit, I have been in many Elmtree stores but have never taken the time to price the stuffed animals; I just assumed that they would be way over-priced. When I picked up a cute, huggable toy made by Fiesta, I could not believe the price. At $8.00 it was well within the range I would pay for an animal that was approx. 14" long. I highly recommend checking out all of the products while visiting these stores. I realize that you are only concerned with collecting Beanie Babies, but it's also time to expand your horizons and look for and experience other product lines.

I have decided to feature two of Mr. Martin's stores in order to show you how they really do have customer service as their number one priority. I spoke with the Manager Mary at Potomac Mills Mall and asked her to explain why her store stood out more so than the others. Her reply was the following:

"I will make up baskets and gift bags upon customers request. My store is located in an outlet mall, at least 25% of the store merchandise is discounted. I hand out customer appreciation cards. I also give 10% off coupons to Seniors, and anyone who may be thinking about making a large purchase in the future. This is an incentive for them to come back using their 10% off coupons, and also a good way of making a new repeat customer. We also offer a large selection of cards, gifts & collectibles, friendly customer service, and make specialty products for customers per their request."

Later, I spoke with Judy at Center Plaza Elmtree:

"I also will make up baskets and gift bags upon customers request. I hand out customer appreciation cards along with 10%-off coupons. We try to please our customers and invite them to come back. We pride ourselves on customer service, and we do take wish lists for Beanie Babies. We offer a large selection of cards, gifts, collectibles, clubs etc. Our store is a little different from the other ones because we have a store attached to us called "Jackie's Teacher Store." This store is full of supplies for teachers, parents, and students."

I would like to thank Mr. Martin for allowing me to interview him and for his honesty.

I would also like to thank Mary and Judy for a job well done. They really know what customer service is all about!!! If you ever happen to run into Mr. Martin, Judy or Mary, please stop and take the time to say "Hi" and "Thank You."

CHAPTER FIVE

Kids' Survey—
Hey Kids, What's Up with Ty?

Most surveys conducted up until this point were answered by adults. I wanted to get the kids' impression of Ty and Beanie Babies and conducted a survey which could only be answered by them. I e-mailed them through members' tables in the different clubs. I also contacted Magan's Beanie Babies and BeanieMom and asked if they would post the survey for viewing on their kids pages. Both sites did post the survey for my article for which I was grateful. The survey generated well over several hundred responses. I was fascinated to read how much kids actually knew about Ty's new policy and what was going on with their Beanie Babies. Along with the responses, I was also receiving short stories about their own personal experiences locating Beanies. Many children were very frustrated, but were not willing to give up collecting. Many indicated that they had personally written to Ty with their own views.

Hey Kids: What's Up with Ty?

This survey was conducted off the Internet. The answers to the following questions were answered by children ages eight through 15. I'd like to personally thank everyone who participated in this survey. Without this input I wouldn't have been able to write the following.

I was compelled to write this article for the following reasons:

1. The enormous amount of e-mail which has been generated from children looking for Beanie Babies.
2. I wanted to capture a child's point of view about Ty and its policies.
3. I wanted to let children express their point of view on subjects by asking questions and allowing them to answer in their own words.
4. I also wanted children to know that all of my stories are for their viewing as well. Sometimes they may seem to appeal only to adults, but in fact they were written for children as well.

I would like to add that, since I had an overwhelming response to this survey, I will only be able to type the top five answers for each question.

QUESTION # 1
What made you decide to collect Beanie Babies?

- ✄ Number one answer—They were cute.
- ✄ They were priced within my limit.
- ✄ Most received some for Christmas and decided they wanted to collect them all.
- ✄ Everybody else at school was collecting them because they were so popular.

✈ Boys and girls could collect them and use their imagination playing with them.

QUESTION # 2
Are you as excited about collecting them now as you were in the beginning?

✈ Number one answer—Most kids have gotten excited since the new releases have been announced.
✈ Some kids say that the excitement has died quite a bit for them because of the lack of Beanie Babies in stores.
✈ Some kids are still excited but find that their parents are getting upset about not being able to find Beanies.

The bottom line is that kids still want to collect them; they just want to be able to find them to collect.

QUESTION # 3
How old are you?

Most of the kids who responded to this survey were between the ages of nine & 15 years.

QUESTION # 4
Normally how long do you have to wait before you can buy your next Beanie Babies due to the lack of shortage?

✈ Number one answer—two months.
✈ Some kids get them sooner because their parents have picked them up for them and given them to the kids for a special treat.
✈ Some kids will turn to the Internet for their Beanie Babies, but their complaint now is that even that source has dried up.

- ✒ Some kids say it has been so long ago that they simply can't remember.
- ✒ A lot of kids' biggest complaint was that by the time they get to the store to get them, they are all sold out.

QUESTION # 5
Why do you think other kids are selling their whole collection of Beanie Babies?

- ✒ Number one answer—Money.
- ✒ Some kids feel that the parents are getting tired of seeing their children collect sets of something that they may never be able to complete their sets with.
- ✒ Kids are getting tired of having to look for them and never finding them.
- ✒ Kids are selling their Beanie Babies because they don't like the adults buying them all.

QUESTION # 6
How do you feel about stores and individuals selling current Beanie Babies at an inflated price?

- ✒ Number one answer—This is wrong, unfair and kids can't afford the higher prices.
- ✒ Some kids say that because of stores raising their prices it doesn't allow the kids to buy as many as they would like.
- ✒ Kids would like to remind store owners and individuals selling Beanie Babies that most kids don't even get $5.00 allowance a week.
- ✒ Several kids knew of Ty's new address so that they could turn store owners in for selling Beanie Babies at an inflated price.

QUESTION # 7
How long do you think this fad will last?

- ✖ Number one answer—through Christmas.
- ✖ Some kids don't want it to end.
- ✖ Some kids say six months to a year.
- ✖ A lot of kids were undecided.

QUESTION # 8
What do you think about Ty only allowing stores to order once a month and only 36 of each kind?

- ✖ The number one answer—It stinks.
- ✖ Most kids feel that this is what is causing the lack of Beanie Babies. If Ty wants to sell them, then they need to allow the stores to order more of them.
- ✖ A lot of kids feel that if the larger stores like Nordstroms didn't sell Beanie Babies, that the smaller gift shops would be allowed to order more.
- ✖ Some kids just say that it is the stupidest thing they ever heard of.
- ✖ Kids also claim that this ruling makes it impossible to find Beanie Babies and by the time they get to the stores that are lucky enough to get a shipment, they are all gone, Ty needs to allow stores to order MORE! MORE! MORE!

QUESTION # 9
How do you feel about Ty's Beanie Babies going from a kid's toy to an adult's investment?

- ✖ Number one answer—It's cool.
- ✖ Some kids say that's why they can't find Beanie Babies, the adults are buying them all up.
- ✖ Other kids say that if it wasn't for the adults, they wouldn't have as many Beanie Babies as they do now.

✍ Some kids just don't care.

✍ My favorite answer was—Adults are weird, you never know what they will do next!

QUESTION # 10
Do you plan to still try hunting down Beanie Babies and buying them in the future?

✍ The number one answer—We will buy them as long as Ty makes them.

✍ Some kids say it is very discouraging to try to buy the ones they need from the secondary markets; they simply can not afford the prices.

Kids don't mind who collect Beanie Babies as long as they can go into their favorite store and purchase the ones they want. They are really confused as to why there is such as shortage. One kid asked me if I knew of any other collectible (Toy) that kids and adults collected together. I really couldn't think of any.

As an adult I realize that Ty has been overwhelmed by the popularity of their Beanie Babies and they are trying to produce them as rapidly as possible. I just hope that their judgment won't be clouded by offers from others jumping on the band wagon. The small gift shops and the kids are what got Ty where they are today, and I hope that they will be able to produce more product so that the stores will be able to buy more and the kids can go back to collecting their Beanie Babies.

CHAPTER SIX

June 3rd News Flash

A re you as confused as I am? Maybe this will explain. In the past couple of weeks I have received numerous amounts of e-mail pertaining to Ty and questions about shipments. Some of the e-mail I received stated the following.

"Ty promised us a shipment by June 1, when I contacted Ty I was told there was nothing in the warehouse. My last shipment was on the first part of April, any clue as to what is going on?"

I also received an e-mail from a McDonalds store employee, stating that Ty and McDonalds had signed another deal and that Teenie Beanies would be back in November. I have heard that the new releases have made their way to a few stores. Although I was glad to hear this news what I heard after that is what concerned me. I have been told, and have gotten messages myself from individuals offering to sell the new releases for $30 to $35 each.

I have been told from store owners nationwide that Ty has established a new 800 number for customers and store owners to contact them. Many store owners report that they wait over 30 to 40 minutes before they can get through. This has angered the retailers.

These e-mail messages along with many others made me decide to do further investigating. I wanted to understand what was going on and why these things were happening. I contacted a couple of Canadian stores which sell Beanie Babies, and they both claim that they are experiencing the same problems as the Americans. Many Canadians felt that Ty Canada worked well with them in the past, and they often wondered if the stories they had heard about the States were true.

I then contacted seven individual stores from the East Coast to the West Coast. I spoke with one store owner who told me in order to keep her customers happy she was purchasing her Beanie Babies from other stores that were lucky enough to receive them.

After sitting back and digesting all of this information I decided it was time to call Ty. When I called their 800 number I got a recording that stated due to the volume of calls received that my wait would be approximately one to three minutes. Much to my surprise, I only had to wait eight minutes. I spoke with a customer service representative and informed her who I was and why I was calling.

The following questions were asked and answered accordingly:

Why is Ty concentrating on areas where Beanie Babies are not as popular instead of shipping them to areas where customers have started collections?

Everybody is treated equally.

Why are stores being told orders from 60 days ago would be shipped on June 1st, but now are being told that the warehouse is empty?

Sometime in June all backorders will be shipped. This includes orders for January, February, and March.

I was under the impression that any orders which remained in the system as of April 1st, 1997 were to be considered canceled. Would you please explain this?

Everybody seems to be confused about this new policy. It states that all orders will be canceled except for the last order submitted for each of these months. For example, if you had a store which placed seven orders for the month, all orders would be canceled except for the last one received. As our new policy reflects one order a month and only 36 of each kind as of April 1st 1997.

When do you expect to ship your April and May orders?

Depending on product availability they may be shipped in June or at a later date.

Why would Ty sign a new deal with McDonalds for Teenie Beanies when they haven't even recovered from the last McDonalds deal? (Stores didn't receive shipments for 60 days before the April McDonalds deal started.)

I'm not sure what you are talking about. I'm unaware of any deal between Ty and McDonalds. I'm not saying it's not going to happen…I'm just saying I'm simply unaware of it.

The customer service representative also informed me that Ty has once again just opened up another warehouse, larger than the last one. She also informed me that Ty has updated their computers in order to help meet with demand.

It is beyond me as to why Ty would even consider entering into any other type of licensing agreement with anyone at this time. Although many of us enjoyed collecting the Teenie Beanies, and if given the opportunity would do it again. I'd rather see Ty concentrate more on producing only regular size Beanie Babies.

"What happened to the little kid idea?" Have the adults taken over? "Are Beanie Babies so scarce that individuals are trying to capitalize on collectors by selling the new releases for 30 to 35 dollars? And if so, who is to blame?"

Once again, if Ty would make more Beanies, life would be BEANIE HEAVEN.

Ty's playful cats having a ball. Snip, Zip, Nip and Flip

Beanie Christmas Center piece displaying, Bumble, Caw, Rex, Kiwi and Garcia.

CHAPTER SEVEN

Black Market Beanies

The following article was written to make buyers aware of greedy retailers not only at the local stores, but also on the Internet. I, personally have experienced many situations regarding Beanie Babies, but the two in this article are simply about greedy individuals. Many stores on the Internet deliver what they promise. On the other hand, I have ordered from stores and never received my products, nor an explanation why. I caution collectors to check both your sources thoroughly. Many are misleading and, just because something is advertised for a certain price, it doesn't always mean that's the price you will end up paying. Many sites post falsified information to grab the collectors attention. Once they have it, and you make your inquiry, they change the information by saying it was posted incorrectly or the Beanies have been retired. I'd like to know what school they went to for psychic abilities!!! As far as I know, the only one who knows which items will be retiring is the Ty Company. The fact of the matter is, Ty Warner is probably the only man with this privileged information until the very last minute. Please don't misunderstand me. There are plenty of Internet sites that are very reputable and, if you surf the Internet, you probably know by now which ones they are.

Buyers: Beware of Current
Black Market Inflated Beanie Babies

In April I contacted a very popular site on the Internet about purchasing some Beanie Babies. This site offered quite a few current Beanie Babies including Garcia. I called the 800 number to place my order and was told that I was only allowed to order via the web site. I asked if I could leave my credit card number with them at this time because I did not feel comfortable posting it across the Internet. I was told I had to post it on the web page. I accessed the web page and placed my order. The prices on the page stated $5.95 plus shipping; this included Garcia. A few hours later I received a message from this web site stating that Garcia was $50!!! I replied to ask why. Garcia had not been retired at this point and their price stated $5.95. I also reminded them that this could be considered fraud which would not be good for business. The message I received was Garcia was retired and as soon as the server updated the page, this would be reflected. I replied back informing them of Ty's new policy about selling current Beanie Babies at an inflated price. Needless to say I never heard from them, nor did I get my shipment!

I have also been getting reports about stores getting in the new releases and then selling them for anywhere from $15 to $50...In my opinion, they are simply taking advantage of the Beanie Babie shortage and are trying to make extra money at their customer's expense. But what they don't know will hurt them. I decided to check out a few of these stories for myself. I visited a store that had several retired Beanies on consignment, but also had a few of the current releases on consignment as well. I inquired how this operation worked. I was told that either the store manager or an outside customer had purchased these items and then displayed them as consigned goods. I informed them of Ty's policy concerning current Beanie Babies; they didn't seem to be at all fazed by it.

I called Ty's customer service number and spoke with a Customer Service Representative. I explained what I had experienced and asked if this was against their policy, (as I knew it was). I was told that Ty, Inc. would appreciate it if any customer feels that any store is engaging in inflated prices for current Beanie Babies for the customer to contact Ty directly.

Please furnish the following information, if available, and mail it to the following address:

Ty, Inc.
Complaint Dept.
PO Box 5377
Oakbrook, IL 60522

Send: Store name and address.
Phone number, if possible.

Also, state what price the current Beanie Babies are being sold for. The more information the better!!

I am a Beanie collector, and I will admit that I have paid more than $6.00 for current ones, as well as $30 for a retired piece. Retired pieces can be sold for any amount of money...they are considered secondary market prices, but current ones can only be sold up to the limit that Ty has specified. I did read an article which stated that current pieces could be sold up to $7.50, but this depends on the area that you purchase them in. I also asked the Ty representative about the highest price at which stores could sell current pieces. I was told that it really depended on location because Ty sold them to different locations at different prices. She would not offer any more than that. I assume that they are

referring to Canada where the money exchange is higher...
This is my opinion.

My advice is to anyone who reads this article and finds
that this situation is happening in their hometown, contact
Ty and let them know. Maybe if they can put a stop to this
madness, we will all be able to find and purchase Beanie
Babies at a reasonable price.

CHAPTER EIGHT

Interview with the Most Popular Beanie Web Sites

From the moment I started searching the Internet for Beanie Babies I have been intrigued about the people who work behind the scenes of these Web Sites. What was the driving factor that make them spend many hours in front of a keyboard. I realized that we will probably never have the opportunity to meet these individuals. I wanted to know more!!!

I contacted several different variety sites and asked if they would be interested in helping me write an article featuring themselves and their Web Sites. I then compiled a list of questions and sent it to them. Once the questions were answered, I compiled all of the information into an article. A lot of my questions were answered and I hope yours will be as well.

Behind the Scenes of the Most Popular Web Sites
- The Beanie Babies Buddies Club
- The BeanieMom

- ⚮ Lemon Lainey's Site
- ⚮ Magan's Site
- ⚮ R.J.W.'s Beanie Mania

I would like to personally thank the following:

- ⚮ Beanie Baby Buddies Club—Beanie Master Mr. Randy Jones
- ⚮ BeanieMom—Sara Nelson
- ⚮ Lemon Lainey—Kevin & Elaine
- ⚮ Magan's Beanie Babies—Magan's Beanie Mom, Beanie Dad, and all of its volunteers
- ⚮ RJW's Beanie Mania—Wendy Malcom

I appreciate their taking the time to answer these questions for this article. Why not make it a point to stop by their sites and thank all of them for a job well done?!!!!

I hope you enjoy reading this article as much as I've enjoyed writing it. I also hope that some of your questions will be answered. I know mine have!

BBB Club Survey Results

Please provide your site name and location:

http://www.netreach.net/~rjones/beanie.html
The Beanie Babies Buddies Club.

Please provide a short Bio on yourself.

My name is Randy Jones, and I was born in a old log cabin on the banks of the Mississippi where I grew up learning to read by candlelight. No…wait…that was Abe Lincoln. I was first released to 3-D conciousness on Remulak, 22,330 Galactic standard. This is my first contact with a sentient species. Resistance is Futile! No…wait…that's not it either…OK…how about this. Born 1951 near Philadelphia, Pa., USA. After a bunch of kid stuff, I graduated from the University of North Carolina, where I was an active member of the Peace movement, which ran concurrent with the Vietnam War. We lost both the movement and the War. Bummer. Got married in '77, and have been in love with the same woman for over 20 years. (Sure hope my wife doesn't find out.) We have twin girls (9), and stopped there with kid production. We still live in the Philadelphia area, and will probably be here forever. It's not that we like it here all that much, it's just that putting all our STUFF into boxes and shipping it to another place just to unpack it again seems too much like work to all of us! Avid interests are fishing (saltwater), and of course, computers. I prefer to build any system I use by myself. That probably explains why only half my equipment works at any one time. I plan to live to be 104 years old.

How long have you been operating this site?

We first hung out the Beanie-Shingle 11/1/96.

What gave you the idea to dedicate your time to a Beanie Baby web site?

See (TWINS) above. It wasn't really an idea…more like a demand from the three women that live here too!!!

Do you visit other sites to check out information, and if so which ones?

Now there's a sore point. I don't get out NEARLY as often as I should. Spend too much time working on things here at the old home site. When I DO get out, it's always a necessity to check Kims, Lemon Lainey, BeanieMom, Magan's, or RJW's. Usually, somebody hits me over the head with a 2" x 4" and gets me to go look at a specific page for something I should be aware of...

Approximately how many hours a day do you work with your site? Please explain.

Thankfully, it's down to several hundred hours a day. Of course, now that things are running pretty smoothly, it's more "tweaking" little items and answering E-mail than anything else. Adding new members eats up a pretty decent chunk of time... we're probably going to add another 500 or so all too soon!

How many people help you operate your site?

Three people (my wife, JD, and Molly McLay) con-tribute heavily to new materials and error correction (see Molly McLay). I do all of the coding, scanning, uploading etc. of anything that you see on the site.

Have you seen activity increase or decline in the last couple of months? Please explain.

Things peaked several weeks before Easter, '97, as far as I was concerned. It was at that time that TY ran into all of their distribution/reorganization problems. Since then the growth rate has been slower, but much steadier in terms of people visiting the sites. Then again, there are hundreds more BB sites out there now than there were when we first started in the fall of '96!

How has Ty's guidelines for web sites affected you?

Didn't pay too much attention to it, since we're non-commercial. Added a few ® or ™ symbols to the BB name, but that's about it.

What type of information does your site contain?

NOW you're talking!!! Heck...if we don't have it, you don't want it!!!! We have a decent Guestbook, Forum for posting messages, Chat, Group mail to all club members, a game zone, articles by the one and only JD, activities to download, as well as links to many of the major and minor BB sites out there on the web.

Approximately how many e-mails a day do you receive?

A quiet day—10...a busy day—100.

What is the most popular question you get asked from people visiting your site?

"Can I join your club...Please, oh Please, can I join your club?" Many request help getting some code correct for their personal webpages.

What type of complaints are people lodging about Ty or Beanie Babies?

Just one: THERE AREN'T ANY BEANIES ANYWHERE!!!!!!

How long do you anticipate operating your site?

3 years, 6 months, 2 days, 25 hours, 30 mintues AND 16 seconds.

How long do you think this fad will last?

Tough call. At this level of fervor...maybe thru Christmas, but I think there will be Beanies around for years to come! A lot will depend on the secondary market.

BeanieMom Survey Results

Please provide your site name and location.

The BeanieMom NetLetter—
http://www.beaniemom.com

Please provide a short Bio on yourself.

I am 36 years old. I have a husband, Chris and three daughters.

How long have you been operating this site?

I began the site with a partner named Ginger in October, 1996.

What gave you the idea to dedicate your time to a Beanie Baby web site?

My children were just beginning their Beanie Baby collection and my husband thought I should develop a web page. I decided to merge our love of Beanies with the desire to learn about web page development. I wanted to create an enjoyable web site where all individuals could learn more about Beanies and share their stories, experiences, etc.

Do you visit other sites to check out information, and if so which ones?

I do not have the time to surf as much as I would like. The sites I most visit are the Ty web page, Kim & Kevin's and Magan's web page.

Approximately how many hours a day do you work with your site? Please explain.

I typically work at least six hours a day on the site. I have a laptop in the kitchen and another in my bedroom. Between the two, I can work on the page throughout the day. With school ending shortly, I am not certain I will be able to maintain that many hours on the page daily.

How many people help you operate your site?

I have six primary individuals who contribute to the site. However, the BeanieMom site is mainly a site for others to share their stories, etc., so I have many BeanieMoms, BeanieDads, and BeanieKids that help shape the page and make it as much fun as it is.

Have you seen activity increase or decline in the last couple of months? Please explain.

I have seen a rapid growth in the site which corresponds with the growing interest and collectibility of Beanies themselves. As more individuals begin collecting, their desire for Beanie information has contributed to the growth of the page.

How has Ty's guidelines for web sites effected you?

I have always tried to operate the BeanieMom site in accordance with the guidelines set forth by the Ty Company. They have created a marvelous product and deserve to have exclusive use of all trademarks.

What type of information does your site contain?

The BeanieMom page has numerous sections of interest for collectors of all ages. Some of the more popular sections are: Collectors Corner, The Beanie Market and Pricing Guide, Net News by Vicky, The Beanie Hunting Stories, Where do you buy your Beanies, the Q&A section by Jeannine and the Beanie articles by Peggy Gallagher.

Approximately how many e-mails a day do you receive?

I receive approximately 250 e-mails a day.

What is the most popular question you get asked from people visiting your site?

I guess the single most common question is individuals asking about the values of their Beanies, in particular mistake Beanies.

What type of complaints are people lodging about Ty or Beanie Babies?

Currently, most individuals are frustrated about how hard it is to find Beanies. They are hoping that local stores will be able to receive regular, complete shipments in the near future.

How long do you anticipate operating your site?

I will continue to operate the BeanieMom site as long as it is fun for myself and my children and it continues to be a positive aspect of our family life.

How long do you think this fad will last?

I do not think Beanie Babies are a fad. I believe there is a well established core group of collectors that will continue to maintain the interest in and market for current and retired Beanies. I also believe that Beanies are such a great toy from a non-violent, educational aspect that children will continue to desire them for years to come.

Lemon Lainey Survey Results

Please provide your site name and location.

Lemon Lainey Design
http://www.lemonlaineydesign.com Windsor, Berkshire, England, Great Britain

Please provide a short Bio on yourself.

Elaine Smith ("Lemon Lainey!") is a freelance graphic designer and photographer who started collecting Beanie Babies in 1993, the first one being Patti the Platypus! Her husband, Kevin is the website programmer/developer and his work includes writing all the CGI programs behind the automated auctions run on the website. They spend most of their evenings and weekends ensuring that the information and photographic images of the Beanie Babies are kept accurate and updated.

How long have you been operating this site?

Since October/November 1996…however, the web counter only started on 09-December-96! The site receives over 25,000 hits per day, however, the counter only registers hits on the index page at the moment, we hope to sort this out soon to collect all the hits!

What gave you the idea to dedicate your time to a Beanie Baby web site?

We love the Beanie Babies so much and we have made so many fantastic friends who collect them…we have lovely comments from our customers and website visitors and we really really enjoy taking the photographs of them in their "natural surroundings"!

Do you visit other sites to check out information, and if so which ones?

Yes, we do…usually…BeanieMom's, Magan's Beanie Babies in Canada, Bears By the Sea (pricing guide), Ty Inc. home page (of course!), JT Puffins, Madison, Wisconsin, Beanie Babies Buddies Club, and Libearty does London (this is the best ever…fab site, must see!!!!!)

Approximately how many hours a day do you work with your site? Please explain.

Elaine approx. seven hours every day…Mainly on auctions, dealing with e-mails, website design, photography, packaging beanies and mailing. Kevin: approx. five hours every day, after coming home in the evening, on weekends, writing programs, updating information, implementing new pages, and site maintenance.

How many people help you operate your site?

Just the two of us!

Have you seen activity increase or decline in the last couple of months? Please explain.

Increase, for sure...there are loads more collectors coming online than ever before. When we first started there were only a few websites...maybe 10 max. that we knew of...and we did a lot of searching...now you can't move for them!!!! Hopefully we established our name and reputation early on!!

How has Ty's guidelines for web sites effected you?

We received a letter from their lawyers in the UK asking us to ensure that there were no tags or labels showing anywhere on our site, which meant that we had to retake all our photographs, or digitally remove the tags on the images themselves...and also to add a disclaimer/non-affiliation clause from Ty Inc. to say that we are not connected in any way...This caused us no real problems, only that we have to explain to people that all our Beanies are genuine and do have all their tags attached, they just don't show in the photos on the website!

What type of information does your site contain?

Complete list and photographs of all the Beanie Babies ever created—extremely popular! Auctions of retired and redesigned Beanie Babies (each week). Beanie Baby Links page (Beanie website owners can add their own links!) Auction Winners page, which gives an idea of average value as price guide. Information pages (always being updated), Lemon Lainey's Trading Post (widely used), Lemon Lainey's Guestbook (widely used), New and Retired Beanie Babies announcements as soon as we hear!

Approximately how many e-mails a day do you receive?

> About 150-300! Not always easy to reply to all of them...we've ended up having standard replies to the questions that crop up most often!

What is the most popular question you get asked from people visiting your site?

> "Can we buy the British Beanie like Libearty/Maple?" ...Lemon (Elaine) is in contact with the Managing Director of Ty UK, who told her—this has not yet been produced, possibly it will be by the end of 1997...!

What type of complaints are people lodging about Ty or Beanie Babies?

> Lack of distribution...not making them fast enough!...signing up contracts with big stores and not looking after the little ones...and not listening to the kids!

How long do you anticipate operating your site?

> Hopefully, always!!!! We just love the Beanies so much that hopefully Ty will keep on producing them always...we're wondering how long it'll be before they run out of species!!!! We've now joined up with a UK company called the Velveteen Bean Bear Company who does not have it's own website and we shall shortly be selling these for retail prices...they are the cutest little Bean Bears that are dressed in traditional British/European clothing...some of these are Beefeaters, Guardsman, Scotsman, Frenchman, Policeman, Golfer, Chauffeur, Cook, Jockeys,

Ty's Congo and Bongo just hanging around.

We are the bears of the world. Teddy,
Maple, Garcia, Curley and Liberty.

Digger, Claude, Goldie, Coral and Bubbles.

Fisherman, Country Gentleman etc. etc. The first part of this page is at http://www.lemonlaineyde-sign.com/velveteen.html—we hope that collectors all over the world will want to build up a collection of these...we love doing photos of these too! This page will be continually updated.

How long do you think this fad will last?

We have been told that it'll be another three to five years, however, so long as Ty does not behave like the company who made the "Cabbage Patch Kids," then we think that this could be true...we think realisti-cally about another two years, provided Ty plays it's cards right and doesn't run out of animals to make!!! Or we might end up with fruit and vegetable beanies (now there's an idea...I'm sure a Lemon would go down a treat!!!!)
Elaine & Kevin Smith
Lemon Lainey Design
England, UK
Website : http://www.lemonlaineydesign.com/

Magan's Survey Results

About my website:
The Website is updated by Magan, Beanie Baby Dad (who is also the webmaster), and Beanie Baby Mom. Mom started my collection of Beanie Babies with the purchase of Garcia the tie-dye bear at a hotel gift shop while on vacation last year. Mom and I are the tireless hunters of those elusive Beanie Babies in the gift shop jungle. Dad knows all this HTML stuff and provides support for all this content. Many of the pages are designed using common application packages like MS Office 97 and Netscape. I'm (Meg-hanne) the collec-tor of many different Beanie Babies including all of

the most recent retired Beanie Babies. I pick out the graphics and we all provide content for the pages. There are also the efforts of volunteers who provide the really neat map and guestbook (John), and others who provide many of the news stories you read on my main page (index.html). The success of the site is dependent on the volunteers and readers who visit my pages frequently. It is a time-consuming hobby; however, it is also fun to hear from others providing those hot tips on Beanie Babies. Beanie Hugs! Magan, Beanie Baby Mom, Beanie Baby Dad.

How long have you been operating this site?

Since around January, 1997.

What gave you the idea to dedicate your time to a Beanie Baby web site?

Two hobbies combined (Beanies and Computers).

Do you visit other sites to check out information, and if so which ones?

Yes, my favorite one is BeanieMom's Web Site which has tons of information on Beanie Babies. I also visit Rosie's, Kim's, Bears By the Sea, LeAnne's, Suzanne's, and several others.

Approximately how many hours a day do you work with your site?

One hour or less.

Please explain.

Most of the work is done by volunteers for the page

updates. Very little of the content actually comes from me. Many visitors contribute stories, news, and information you see on the pages.

How many people help you operate your site?

At least a dozen at any given time. Many volunteers help to update certain pages or areas of the site.

Have you seen activity increase or decline in the last couple of months? Please explain.

Some decline. There are many more Beanie web sites to choose from for first time visitors. It is easy to get lost in the search engines. There also seems to be a declining interest due to the difficulty in finding Beanie Babies at stores.

How has Ty's guidelines for web sites effected you?

It will cause many hours of work to bring the site up to their standards.

What type of information does your site contain?

News, history, lists, retailer information, accessories, and many other areas. It has grown to over 50 web pages over time and includes links to many other valuable resources.

Approximately how many e-mails a day do you receive?

Around 10 to 15 a day. Used to be much more before adding links to FAQs. It is difficult to answer every note. Dad reviews all incoming mail (due to unpredictable content) and distributes to volunteers or me.

What is the most popular question you get asked from people visiting your site?

"Where can I find Beanie Babies?"

What type of complaints are people lodging about Ty or Beanie Babies?

Inability to meet demand and reactions to new policies.

How long do you anticipate operating your site?

No plans to quit as long as there is an interest by visitors.

How long do you think this fad will last?

The popularity may be a fad; however, I believe there will always be a select group who are interested in collecting Beanie Babies. So if the popularity wanes, hold on to those Beanie Babies because they will become more popular at a later point.

R.J.W.'s Beanies Survey Results

Please provide your site name and location.

R.J.W.'s Beanie Mania http://www.beaniemania.com

Please provide a short Bio on yourself.

My name is Wendy Malcolm. I am 30 something and a mom of two beautiful children! Jessica is three and Jordan is six months. My husband Rob and I run a Hallmark card shop and convenience store, as well as our website. We both graduated from the University of Guelph, Ontario, Canada in 1987 (wow a long time ago!!) which is where we met. We live in the country on a farm we purchased in July and after a lot of hard work, I am happy to call it home. We have three American Cocker Spaniels who were our 'babies' until Jessie and Jordie. Oh, and I can't forget, two cats, Jack a huge orange tabby, and Barney, a grey and white kitty, whose mommy abandonded him in the barn when we first moved here.

How long have you been operating this site?

Just over two years, although the domain site is new.

What gave you the idea to dedicate your time to a Beanie Baby web site?

Two years ago when we first went on line we were primarily a stuffed teddy bear site. After being up for about five months we started to receive oodles of mail from Beanie collectors in Illinois, this expanded to Georgia soon after. About a year later I was spending hours answering mail and trying to find info for people on Beanies. We decided that since so much of my time was spent dealing with Beanies and Beanie info, that we should dedicate the site to Beanies. And the result is what you see today.

Do you visit other sites to check out information, and if so which ones?

Yes, most certainly! TY's page, Magan's Beanie News, BeanieMom Netletter and Kim's Beanie Site are four that I visit the most frequently.

Approximately how many hours a day do you work with your site? Please explain.

48 hours a day! A lot of time! We had to put Jessie in daycare so that I could keep up with e-mail and updating of the site. I start around nine every morning and work through until five. Then when the kids are in bed, around eight, I am back in front of the computer until usually around three or four am. I think the largest part of my time is spent answering e-mail. And I still fall behind. The rest is spent setting up new scripts to run on the site, searching for new things to add, and trying to keep on top of the news, mailing list, chat room, and the various other aspects of the site. Gabi has really helped tons since she started her pages. It has relieved some pressure to not have to search for what the latest news is and Gabi does a fantastic job!

How many people help you operate your site?

Just me. Gabi writes all her news releases in e-mail form and I add them to her site.

Have you seen activity increase or decline in the last couple of months? Please explain.

Activity is increasing. There are new people exposed to Beanies all the time it seems. People from states I have never heard from before are 'coming out of the woodwork' it seems!

How has Ty's guidelines for web sites effected you?

Although we have not received any official notification from TY themselves, we have removed all TY's logos from our site. As well, I have removed all the pictures I spent hours scanning from the cataolgues off our site. Soon to be replaced with pictures we have taken ourselves and are sitting here waiting to be scanned, when I have a minute.

What type of information does your site contain?

We have a number of different collector lists that have been requested over the last six months and Gabi's pages include 1) Announcements of various Beanie news stories, 2) Rumour breaking in an attempt to keep new collectors up to date on who is and isn't retired and 3) Nightmares where people can share their Beanie hunting experiences. Gabi also has a Retailer Web Ring so visitors can find sites that sell easier and we plan to add an Internet Consumer Watchdog page to help promote those who are good to deal with and warn of those who are not.

Approximately how many e-mails a day do you receive?

Between 200 and 300 on average, with the majority coming on Friday, Saturday and Sunday.

What is the most popular question you get asked from people visiting your site?

"Can you sell me Maple or put me on a waiting list?"

What type of complaints are people lodging about Ty or Beanie Babies?

The main concern I hear is the lack of availability.

How long do you anticipate operating your site?

As long as people still visit we will still have a site!

How long do you think this fad will last?

That's a hard one. Personally I think Beanies are here to stay. They may not be the rage they are at this time, but I think they have staying power. With the large variety of animals and the oodles of possibilities to come, TY has more than a Fad here. I think the demand will level off but remain right up there with toys like Hot Wheels and Barbie.

CHAPTER NINE

Secondary Market

The secondary market was rapidly gaining attention. Just about anyone who needed Beanie Babies in a hurry always ended up buying them through this market.

Although it would be nice to be able just go into a store and purchase Beanie Babies like we did in the good old days, it seems as though those days are behind us for the time being. The main attraction the secondary market holds is simply, "They have what we want!!!!"

I received responses to this survey from people whose ages ranged from nine to 44 years of age. I also received this information from 18 different states.

What do you know about the Secondary Market?

One eleven-year-old summed it up this way. "The Secondary Market is where you can go and buy Beanies for a much higher price but at anytime and anywhere."

A sixteen-year-old had this following comment. "I know that there are a lot of Secondary Market places on the Internet and I know that as Beanie Babies become more rare, the Secondary Market transactions increase (as well as the price per Beanie)."

A 35-year-old woman had this to say. "The Secondary Market is the people who buy Beanies solely to resell them at higher prices. I dislike the Secondary Market and feel that this market is the reason my seven year old can't find any Beanies when she goes to the store with her allowance money."

My favorite was the following; it says it all. This was sent to me by a 44-year-old women from Illinois: "I believe the Secondary Market in relation to Beanies is any Beanie sale or purchase by an individual OR retailer where any profit money (or loss) is not going directly to Ty. A Beanie can only be sold once by Ty, who makes a profit on the primary sale of the Beanie to a retailer. Examples I see of Secondary Market sales are individuals selling Beanies to other individuals over the Internet, antique stores selling retired Beanies and/or Canadian Beanies, and individuals selling at group sales or trade shows.

I have no problem whatsoever with a Secondary Market situation! I'm not saying I LIKE IT, but this is a free market economy. When you have a desirable product, but then limit its distribution, this will only encourage greater demand for that product. And to have that, the retiring of Beanies, (i.e., greater scarcity), how can a Secondary Market be prevented? I believe many people will hoard the Beanies they buy and introduce them on the Secondary Market upon their retirement, or rumors of great scarcity of the Beanies (for example, Spooky).

It's all supply and demand. The only way to stop the Secondary Market is for Ty to flood the primary market with Beanies, which would probably be the end of the Beanie-Mania. When Beanies would be readily available, the secondary market would die a slow death due to lack of profit. Perhaps retired Beanies only will retain Secondary Market Value.

Why do you feel that the Secondary Market is taking over?

Many people feel it is because of the money that is able to be made on the Secondary Market. Others claim that store owners are just tiring of the whole Beanie scene and want to continue to make quick cash, but instead of dealing with local customers (whom may be rude), are simply choosing to sell in large quantities to the Secondary Market. A lot of this was mentioned in the survey results.

Of course there are always two sides to every coin. Most kids answered in this manner.

Beanies are becoming harder to find. Their popularity continues to increase and when the demand is high and the supply is low, the people on the Secondary Market who are only out to make a profit can charge high prices for them.

I don't like the fact that the Secondary Market is taking over. Mother won't allow me to purchase from these people who she calls "money-grabbers."

Who do you feel is to blame for this?

Kids' point of view!!
Many kids blame the lack of supply for creating the secondary market.

This statement comes from an 11-year-old girl from Virginia: "I think that greedy adults are to blame for buying up all the $5.00 Beanies and selling them to make money."

This statement was made by a 12-year-old girl from Alabama: "Ty for not making enough and the grown-ups for having more money than sense."

Adult version:
The situation for high-priced Secondary Market sales certainly begins with Ty's marketing policies. Limited distribution for a high demand product. This sets the stage for greed and dishonesty by some retailers.

A 35-year-old male from California had this to say: "If you want to deal on the Secondary Market, then do so. If you don't, then don't. I think you should own up to your own actions and stop laying blame. This is a free country and you're free to make your own decisions. Along with that you are free to be held accountable for those decisions."

Would you consider purchasing on the Secondary Market and why?

Kids' version:
11-year-old from California: "I will purchase from the Secondary Market because I only need a few and those are the ones which are really hard to find."

13-year-old from New Jersey: "I have purchased from the Secondary Market. It was back in January. I had just started collecting and I needed Liberty. My experience was good; I just had to wait a while to get him."

13-year-old from Illinois: "I think it's dumb to buy from the Secondary Market, but someone that's really Beanie-Nuts, (like my mom and some of her friends) are considering it."

Adult version:
41-year-old Michigan woman says: "If I could get what I needed (for a sad daughter) for a reasonable price I might. Only because I have pounded the pavement every day for two months and have been unable to buy any."

35-year-old woman from New Jersey says: "No, I would not buy from the Secondary Market—I distrust unknown individuals who are not affiliated with a reputable store, and I honestly don't believe that any doll or toy, no matter how cute, is worth the kind of money that the Secondary Market is generating."

If you have ever purchased from the Secondary Market what was your experience?

Kids' version:
14-year-old from Kentucky: "I have bought current Beanies from the Secondary Market for $13.00 only because I could not find them. It's kind of scary to think that's what they go for."

13-year-old from Illinois: "I have purchased from the Secondary Market a lot of times and everything turned out OK. The most I ever paid was $30.00 for Digger because he was retired. My cheapest one was Seaweed for $8.00."

13-year-old girl from Illinois: "I've never purchased from the Secondary Market, never wish to, but it probably will happen."

Adult version:

41-year-old from Michigan: "I have bought over the Internet and did receive things fine. Only a few because of the prices—too high. Crazy for a $5.00 toy. Takes the fun out of it."

44-year-old woman from Illinois: "Internet prices overall are reasonable, and you have a choice of who you want to do business with. Beanie sales on the Internet are too competitive to stay high for long. It seems new Beanie sales on the net were about $20.00 to $30.00 a week ago when very few people could even find them in stores. Now people are selling them for $10.00 to $15.00 because more people have them for sale. Personally, I was willing to wait and just found most of them in a store this weekend for $5.00."

Secondary Market Interview

Round Two

A few of my Beanie Babies for my own personal collection were purchased from the secondary market. In most cases I found them to be fair and my purchase arrived as promised. I viewed the Secondary Market, as meeting the supply for a very "BIG" demand.

P&D Collectibles/Snacker's Gift Service

Please tell us a little bit about yourself.

I'm in the educational field and run P&D as a second business.

Please tell us a little bit about how the Secondary Market works.

It is a matter of supply and demand. Many parts of the country do not get a particular product such as Beanie

Babies. The net allows the "haves" to sell to the "have nots." This was also the case with Mattel's Holiday Barbies.

What is it about Beanie Babies that attracted the Secondary Market?

Again, supply and demand. Ty has done a marvelous job of driving interest up with retirements and smart marketing. They do not sell to large chain stores such as Target or Walmart.

What is your highest priced and most popular Beanie Baby?

Garcia was at first at about $55. Now there does not seem to be a clear first choice.

How long do you anticipate this fad lasting?

Until Christmas.

Do you have children who purchase Secondary Market Beanie Babies from you or are they mostly adults?

Mostly adults, but children have purchased.

What makes an item a collectable and who determines the price of that item?

It seems that if someone else has one and you don't, it becomes desirable. I cannot see what makes a Beanie a collectible. It is after all just a bean bag toy. How can it possible endure for years. We'll have to wait and see.

Do you sell current Beanie Babies and, if so, what is their price range?

$12.50-$30

I've noticed that there are a few current Beanie Babies already on the Secondary Market, can you explain this?

It's because of short supply and people who just can't wait to have them. "Be the first on your block." I think children pumping their parents to buy is partly responsible for this.

How do you obtain your Beanie Babie supply to sell on the Secondary Market?

We have spotters who purchase them and then sell them to us.

How long have you been dealing on the Secondary Market?

In Beanies a bit over two months.

What other items do you sell on the Secondary Market?

Barbie dolls.

To date, what is the most popular item you have ever offered on the Secondary Market?

The 1995 Holiday Barbie.

I'm sure, as a dealer of Beanie Babies, you have heard many stories about Ty, Inc. If you had to sum up the company in two sentences or less, what would you say?

My dog, Noel, guarding her Babies.

Caw, Rex and Bumble. "1996 Retired"

Magic and Mystic

"There's no Peter Cotton Tail here."

I find them unwilling to deal with the small "Mom and Pop" stores.

I realize many people purchase from the Secondary Market, but for those people who are skeptical, what would you tell them?

If you have to have it, then buy it. Set a price you can afford that seems reasonable and don't go above it. Also, don't let anyone tell you you'll be able to get it later if you wait. They probably already have it themselves.

What factors could effect the Secondary Market value for Beanie Baby collectors?

Supply. If they become readily available the prices will plummet on them except possibly for retireds.

I have read in my research that the Teenie Beanies have hit the Secondary Market as well. Which one is the most popular and what would a whole set of ten sell for?

Patti is most popular and possibly Pinky. $50 for a set.

Do you have any funny or unusual story you would like to share concerning Beanie Babies?

Just the number of people who thank you over and over again for just having them available. I have very few negative comments.

If customers were interested in purchasing any of your Secondary Market Beanie Babies, how would you prefer that they contact you?

We have an established web site. We have an 800 number, along with regular number and fax number.

We also have an online order form. Any of these is OK with us.

Do you have any other Beanie Baby product line that customers may be interested in knowing about?

Beanie Baby trading cards.

Please feel free to include any extra comments.

It's been fun dealing with Beanies. Hope it lasts.

Fat Cat Cafe

Please tell us a little bit about yourself.

I'm a 24-year-old stay at home mom. I do website design as a profession. Actually, this Beanie thing was a hobby gone crazy.

Please tell us a little bit about how the Secondary Market works.

How I think it should work or how it seems to be working for the Beanie craze? How I THINK it should work is, someone buys an item. That item either becomes rare or retired; others who are looking for it are willing to pay a certain amount for that item over what the retail is. How it SEEMS to be working for the Beanie craze is anyone, (store shop owners who buy direct from Ty, kids, moms, dads, and everyone in between) grabs all the Beanies they can and sells them at high prices. We seem to be losing the retail market in all this Beanie stuff. You can hardly find a place to even buy Beanies at retail anymore. You have to turn to the people who have them, and they all want high prices for them. I mean most of the Beanies I sell are just so I can afford to buy Beanies for myself.

What is it about Beanie Babies that attracted the Secondary Market?

I think the attraction is that Ty slowed down on shipping and people started the "I have to have it now!" thing. The retired and harder-to-find beanies really are rare in mint condition (that's a big plus for the secondary market). There is money to be made and a lot of people know it. People want Beanies and if they can't get them from the stores, they are going to turn to someone else for them.

What is your highest priced and most popular Beanie Baby for sale?

I think if you are talking old-retired, the priciest most-wanted would be Humphrey, the camel. The dinos are expensive, but they are almost affordable at around $250-300, but Humphrey is around $600+ mint and that is stretching it for most people.

How long do you anticipate this fad to last?

Even if Ty starts shipping in September or October on a regular basis the retirement announcements in Dec/Jan are going to start that manic search for all the ones you are afraid may retire and that may drag this frenzy out. But other than that, I give it no more than six months for the secondary market on current Beanies. The old retires may stand on their own for a long time, but there has got to be some point when people just aren't going to pay that much for a Beanie they are still making and should be able to get in a store.

Do you have children who purchase Secondary Market Beanie Babies from you or are they mostly adults?

Actually, I have been doing toy shows and I always end up giving Beanies away to kids or selling them to them at my cost. I think the kids need to be able to get them at reasonable prices. But for the most part, it's the adults who buy from me. They want them in their collection.

What makes an item a collectable and who determines the price of that item?

Availability, demand, how many of that item were made, how many of that item are still available in mint condition. The price is reflected by all those things. Retiring an item helps the collectablity. It becomes something you can never get again at a store.

Do you sell current Beanie Babies and, if so, what is their price range?

My prices at the toy shows have been $12 and up. The average price in my area seems to be about $15 for currents. The price is higher for those hard to find, like the bunnies and Valentino.

I've noticed that there are a few current Beanie Babies already on the Secondary Market, can you explain this?

A few? More like ALL. It's crazy! Store owners are taking stock and selling it right into the secondary market, no Beanies to be found anywhere unless you wait in line for hours and deal with crazy people. The fact that most of the time you can only buy one at a time, has made currents easy prey for the secondary market; no supply and high demand.

How do you obtain your Beanie Babie supply to sell on the Secondary Market?

I started by selling my extras to buy others I needed. I already had them, and it was easy to do. Then, when I found a good deal online, I would buy some to trade or sell to get more I needed. I don't go to stores and buy out the stock. I get all my Beanies from other people who are selling.

How long have you been dealing on the Secondary Market?

With Beanies? About five months. Before then, you could still find them in stores. With collectibles in general a long time. I collect a lot of things, so I am used to having to buy that "one last piece" for my set on the secondary market.

What other items do you sell on the Secondary Market?

At this point nothing! Who has time? Selling Beanies has probably been the most tiring job I have ever taken on as a "hobby." You really have to stay on top of things.

To date, what is the most popular item you have ever offered on the Secondary Market?

Beanie Babies have been the most popular item I have sold. I never really sold many collectibles on the secondary market before Beanies. I did buy and sell a few things, but it was always to finish my sets or collections.

I'm sure, as a dealer of Beanie Babies, you have heard many stories about Ty, Inc. If you had to sum up the company in two sentences or less, what would you say?

Ty Warner has got to be one of the smartest men out there. He knows exactly what he's doing to keep his product in the public eye.

I realize many people purchase from the Secondary Market, but for those people who are skeptical what would you tell them?

The secondary market is just reflecting the demand for Beanies and the fact that there are none out there in stores. Most people don't want to get up at 3:00 in the morning to stand in line just to buy two beanies. The secondary market is the best way to get the Beanie you want with out all of the hassle; someone else has already gone through the hassle for you.

What factors could effect the Secondary Market value for Beanie Baby collectors?

If Ty decides to unretire any of the Beanies, or just plain floods the stores with Beanies, that would make the bottom fall out faster than anything. There's also the chance that people will just get sick of paying high prices and move on to the next collectable they find. That seems like it might happen soon too.

I have read in my research that the Teenie Beanies have hit the Secondary Market as well. Which one is the most popular and what would a whole set of ten sell for?

Pinky and Patti are the most in demand teenies. Their prices are double, if not triple, the other tee-nies. A whole set would cost about $35-40 online, $60-75 offline (I know it sounds crazy, but offline prices are much higher). It's much cheaper to buy a set than to buy each one separately.

Do you have any funny or unusual story you would like to share concerning Beanie Babies?

The only funny thing I find about Beanies is how people take this so seriously. Most of us are here to have fun with something we love and love to collect. There are some people out there who are just too serious about all of this.

If customers were interested in purchasing any of your Secondary Market Beanie Babies, how would you prefer that they contact you?

I use beanies@fatcatcafe.com now.

Do you have any other Beanie Baby product line that customers may be interested in knowing about?

I have been selling *Limited Edition Beanie Baby Trading Cards.* They only made 10,000 sets, so there is a lot of collectability there, and have been selling like hotcakes. A set of 45 cards in a boxed set goes for $24.99 retail, and people love them. Series "B" and "C" are coming out soon, and I already have advance orders for them.

Please feel free to include any extra comments.

I just wanted to say that I have met some wonderful people in "the Beanie world" and am glad I started doing this. But there are those people that need to lighten up. I mean, a bent tag on Peanut isn't the end of the world,...now Humphrey on the other hand (just kidding...ha-ha).

Maple—Canada's Pride and Joy.

CHAPTER TEN

Canadian Viewpoint

A question, which has been asked many times and which I have never been able to answer until now, is "How do the Canadians feel about Ty and their Beanie Babies?"

I had heard so many different stories from Canadians, but was never successful enough to convince any of them to allow me to interview them. It was almost as though they had heard all of the rumors (of which probably only half were true) about the States and Beanie Babies, and they simply did not want to get involved. However, I was lucky enough to contact a very delightful woman who shared her view with me and is now allowing me to share those same views with you.

Would you please state your first and last name?

Carolin Markiewich

What part of Canada are you from?

Sudbury, Ontario which is about six hours north of Niagara Falls, New York, and three hours east of Sault Ste. Marie, Michigan.

Would you please give a Bio on yourself?

I am 32 years old, married with two stepchildren, Tom 12, and Ashley nine. I started Tin Can Alley with my mom about seven years ago and took the business from a part time hobby to a full-time growing concern. I have always been in sales, both retail and wholesale, so I have a in-depth understanding of the business.

When did you start selling Beanie Babies?

My first order was placed in March of this year.

Are Beanie Babies as popular in Canada as you have heard that they were in the states?

I don't know about the rest of Canada, but in Sudbury they haven't become as popular yet, but it's starting.

Ty recently rescinded their 10% plush policy for the States. How have you been effected by this, and was it rescinded for Canada as well?

I had to order regular Ty plush with my initial order, but since then, I have ordered it on my own because it sells so well. However, if I was made to order 10%, I wouldn't be able to continue doing business with Ty.

Does Ty allow the Canadians to sell Beanie Babies, including Maple, to the States?

I don't know exactly what Ty's policy on this is, but I feel that, if Ty didn't want Americans to buy Maple (and the only place Maple is available is in Canada), they wouldn't give Maple so much exposure. For example, the interview between Maple and Quackers, as well as listing Maple as "Our Canadian Friend" on their official checklist.

Do you have a contract with Ty or do you work off purchase orders?

There is no contract. I generally verbally place my orders with my sales Reps.

What do you think caused or started this fad?

Other than the fact that Beanie Babies are adorable I think it is a marketing stroke of genius.

How long do you think this fad will last?

I don't see it ending soon. Beanie Babies appeal to all ages, and, if the average person wants to collect the whole set, it could take years to do so.

I have heard from some people that the Canadian Beanie Babies are plumper. What can you tell us about this, and why do you think they are made differently than from those in the states?

I have heard this also. It's probably because we Canadians don't have the same selection of fat free products that you Americans have.

What is your view on Ty?

I think that Ty, Canada is trying to control a difficult situation. I have heard a lot of ugly rumors about Ty, but I can't make my business decisions from rumors or speculation.

How do they treat the Canadians?

I have had the best treatment from my sales Reps. Stan and Sheila Bernstein (it's because of them that I am selling Beanie Babies) and from my customer service Rep. at Ty, Patrick. I know that they are really busy, but they always make time for me and my questions.

Is Ty true to their word as far as shipments?

No, things are really slow lately, but I received a letter from Ty, Canada thanking me for my patience and telling me that things are going to be better in the future.

Can you get through to them by calling, or do you have to call several times, fax several times etc.?

I have never had to call more than once.

What do you think about Beanie Babies going from a child's toy to a mother's hysteria?

I remember when Tom was into Ninja Turtles. My husband and I went everywhere trying to find them. We all want to give our children the best, and you can't fault parents for that.

How do you feel about Ty selling to the larger stores when they have stated over and over that they would only sell to small gift shops, card shops, hospital gift shops, mom and pop stores, etc.?

As a small business owner I hate it! But as a intelligent human being I can see why they are doing it. I only hope that Ty will make them follow the same restrictions that they have set for us and will make sure that these stores sell them for the same price.

Do you collect Beanie Babies personally?

Of course! Doesn't everybody? The kids love them, even my husband has one.

Did Canada participate in the McDonalds Teenie Beanie promotion?

Yes, Canada's promotion was before the one in the States. It was really popular, so popular that the promotion was cut short because they couldn't keep up with demand.

Has the Secondary market for Beanie Babies hit Canada yet?

I don't know of anyone from Canada that has bought anything from the Secondary Market.

Tell us a little bit about your store and any other specialty items you carry.

Tin Can Alley is all fun. We make our own gourmet popcorn and fudge. We have handmade Truffles (to die for) and gorgeous handmade suckers and candy sticks. We carry Jelly Belly Jelly Beans and a lot of unique candies. We also have a large assortment of gourmet foods that we use to create gift tins with, and a whole lot more!!!!

What items, other than Beanie Babies, are popular in Canada for children to collect?

Basically, anything that is popular in the States becomes popular here too. We get a lot of American TV channels, so our kids see the same commercials.

Is there anything that you would like to comment on for the American customer who may be either coming to Canada for a vacation or seeking to shop in Canada?

I would like to stress the fact that Canadians aren't really any different from Americans. We don't live in Igloos (none that I know of anyway), we don't all speak French (although some do), and we don't always say, "How's it going, eh?" We have the same kinds of stores, the same kinds of cars, and we like doing the same kinds of things. We have some great attractions, some beautiful places, and some really friendly people.

I'd like to thank Carolin for this interview. I contacted a few Canadians to interview; she was the only one who was willing to oblige. I personally plan on checking out some of those Plump Canadian Beanie Babies, and I might even try some of the candy as well.

If you get a chance, why not drop Carolin a line and thank her for giving us all a Canadian's viewpoint on Beanie Babies.

Carolin Markiewich
Tin Can Alley
dmark@isys.ca

CHAPTER ELEVEN

Prototype Bunny

Wouldn't it be nice to not only meet an individual from another country through a story, but then also learn that he has a one-of-a-kind Prototype Bunny?

The Beanie world never ceases to amaze me. Once I think I've got it all figured out, something else happens. Something that only happens once in a lifetime. And, if you just happen to be the lucky soul to discover such a find, not only would it be truly remarkable, it would also be classified as extraordinary.

The Prototype Bunny!!!

I received some information from a source I have worked closely with from time to time. I was told about a gentleman in the UK that claimed he had in his possession a prototype Bunny just like the Bunny we have all come to know as Ty's Floppity Bunny. I was asked to verify the information. Not only was I overwhelmed by the fact that someone of this caliber trusted me to check the information out, but I also was glad to receive a lead. I have always had to go out and either run the roads or stay on the phone all day running up enormous phone bills in order to write my articles. This was the break I needed, and I was grateful for it.

I had no idea how big the story was until I received all of the information. After speaking with Duncan, the owner of the bunny in question, I realized that not only was this extremely interesting, but how Ty handled the whole situation fascinated me. This is the interview conducted with Duncan through the use of e-mail.

Would you please give a bio on yourself?

I am in my fortieth year (a sobering thought), English born and bred, with a lovely wife and two beautiful daughters, aged eleven weeks, and four and a half years. We are very lucky to live in the south of England, not far from London, yet near to the coast and some of the most beautiful, unspoiled countryside that England has to offer.

How did you learn about Beanie Babies and when was the first time you ever laid eyes on one?

A Texan friend who I am in contact with on the Internet through a mutual interest in manned space-flight, e-mailed me one Sunday, approximately four weeks ago, and asked if I could seek out any Beanie Babies which might still be available in the UK. He said that they were extremely collectible in the USA, and that I might be able to find some "retired" examples fairly easily in England, since the craze had not yet developed over here. The next day I made some phone calls, and quickly discovered that the Ty, UK headquarters was only five miles from my home! A helpful sales clerk at Ty told me that all the Beanie

Babies on my friend's list were either "retired," or had never been imported to the UK (like Steg, Bronty and Chilly). Phone calls to UK stockists resulted in the quick realization that I was only exploring territory already well trodden by American collectors, and that any stock of rare and retired Beanies had long since been shipped across the pond! However, I did find a department store with a new shipment of current Beanies, and when I saw them for the first time I was immediately entranced by the little fellows, and began to understand what all the fuss is about.

Which Beanie Baby was your first purchase?

Well, I bought one of each available design in that department store—a total of 24 Beanies! It was, however, the charm of certain individual Beanies which made me start collecting—Bongo and Bessie are particular favorites from that first batch.

I understand that you have found a prototype Beanie. Would you please explain this?

A couple of weeks after I first discovered Beanies, I was in a major London store. They had a number of current Beanies on a shelf, although I quickly discovered that the selection was small, and we already had each of the designs in our collection. In amongst these "regular" Beanies I noticed one single lavender bunny with a large circular ear tag. At first I thought that it must be another type of toy altogether—one that had simply been put on the wrong shelf. On closer inspection I recognized that this must in fact be a Ty Beanie Babie Bunny—it seemed identical in every way to the Floppity I had previously purchased in our very first batch, but nowhere on the tush or ear tags was there any mention of the name Ty. There were various printed headings on the ear tag, and underneath, handwritten in pen, was the phrase "QC Sample," which I took to mean "Quality Control Sample." Intrigued, I bought the Bunny, thinking that it would be well worth the purchase price just to find out his story. The department manager subsequently confirmed that this Bunny could only have come in a shipment from Ty, since his store did not deal in any way with the manufacturer credited on the Bunny's tags (in fact, he had never heard of that particular company!).

How does this prototype compare with Ty's Beanie Babies?

He is virtually identical to the production version of Floppity, except in a few minor ways. The fabric, color, design and method of manufacture (positioning of seams, etc., plastic eyes and nose) are the same as the Ty labeled Bunny. However, he is fractionally larger than the Ty Floppity, is slightly more rounded in the face, with eyes facing forward, rather than slightly sideways, he has a less pointed muzzle, and his neck ribbon is slightly more blue in tone than the production run.

What country is this prototype made in?

He is labeled as being manufactured by a factory in Seoul, Korea.

Can you tell us anything about the company who manufactured the prototype?

Well, yes, but I am nervous about divulging too many details. Their name, Telex number, C.P.O. Box number and Cable address are all clearly printed on the ear tag. The company name and logo are repeated on the tush tag. Ty, UK initially told me that they did not want the name of this Korean supplier made public on the Internet, although this position was to change dramatically later. At the moment I prefer to err on the side of caution, as I do not want to divulge anything that might get me into trouble with Ty's lawyers!

I also understand that you called Ty in regard to this Prototype. Would you please describe their reaction?

I phoned Ty, UK a total of three times. The first time I was simply told by a sales clerk to take Prototype Floppity back to the shop where I had bought him and claim a replacement or a refund!! The second time I asked to speak to the Managing Director, and said that I had been sold what appeared to be a fake Beanie Babie by a reputable retailer! This had the desired effect, and I was immediately put through to Ty UK's Managing Director, Ms. Patricia Roache. I told her the whole story, and read out the details from the ear and tush tags. Ms. Roache immediately said that my Floppity was a prototype sample which should never have got out of the factory, and that Ty would want him back. She asked me what I wanted for him, and suggested a trade for other Beanies. When I asked for things like Quacker without wings, Brownie the Bear and any of the Colored Teddies, Ms. Roache said that not even Ty Warner had such a complete collection, and that my request could not be met! Ms. Roache suggested payment, and when I said that I thought my Prototype Floppity might be worth even more than the $1,500 currently being paid for Brownie the Bear—who after all had a production run of, I believe, 5,000 identical pieces, whilst Proto-type Floppity is unique—Ms. Roache said that she would have to speak to Ty Warner himself, and that she would get back to me. Several hours passed, and I heard nothing, so I phoned Patricia Roache again. This time she told me that the company named on my Floppity's tags had only been under contract to Ty for a short time, that they had only made samples and prototypes which were never intended for sale, and that I was free to auction him for whatever I could get on the Internet!!!

In your opinion how much is this Prototype worth and what do you plan on doing with it?

Prototype Floppity will be auctioned on the Internet, as suggested by Ty, UK itself. He is worth what some-one is prepared to pay for him. No more and no less. Clearly he is not like a normal Floppity toy, and is a unique collector's item. He should go to someone who will appreciate and cherish him for what he is. I really believe that my Prototype Floppity is the "Holy Grail" of Beanie collecting. He is a one-of-a-kind and I feel very privileged to have been lucky enough to have found him. Obviously, I hope that he is worth a lot of money to someone, and would be surprised if his auc-tion price did not exceed that which Brownie the Bear achieves—around $1,500 currently. He could go for a lot more, or, of course, he could go for a lot less. It just depends what someone is prepared to offer.

Have you tried or do you intend to try to locate more prototype Beanies?

I am always on the look-out for rare and collectible Beanie Babies. However, I realize that finding "Pro-totype Floppity" was probably a once in a lifetime chance, and no-one could hope to achieve such a find twice. Our collection currently stands at 55 different Beanie Babies after only four weeks. I would be very happy just to be able to complete our own collection of Beanie Babies; which, incidentally we have cut the tags off and are played with by the children regularly. That is what Beanie Babies are really about—charming children's playthings, although Prototype Floppity is obviously something else, and still has his tags firmly attached!!

If collectors are interested in viewing this Prototype Beanie where can they go to do so?

My friends, Kevin and Elaine Smith are currently setting up a special page as a subsection of their Lemon Lainey Design website. Photographs of "Prototype Floppity" and his tags (albeit with the factory name and details electronically blurred) will be available on that site. I'll give you full details of the address, once the page is ready.

Do you sell Beanies? If so, how can collectors reach you for pricing and availability?

Yes, I sell rare and retired Beanies on-line. I have scoured the countryside and bought as many rare and retired as possible in the hope of making our collection self-financing by selling duplicates. So far I have been singularly unsuccessful and have spent over £700 ($1,120) and not sold one single Beanie! I guess I wasn't cut out to be a businessman! Duncan's On-Line Beanie shop is accessed via Lemon Lainey Designs website. All Beanies are at a fixed price (NOT auctioned, except for Prototype Floppity). The address is http://www.lemonlaineydesign.com/duncan/beanieshop.html

Please feel free to add any extra comments at this time.

What can I say? After only four weeks collecting Beanies I had the very good fortune to find a unique example which should never have left Korea. I really am a lucky man. I would also like to mention the date on the Prototype Floppity's ear tag. The numbers 96.11.14 are handwritten against the printed "198" (Clearly visible in Lemon's photo). I assume that 198 is the standard tag prompt for the date to be inserted, and that it has not been updated since the eighties. I think that it is fair to assume that 96.11.14 is a date, and would relate to 14th November 1996. This is particularly significant since the pastel Bunnies were not launched until January 1997!!!!

My friends, Ricky in Texas and Elaine and Kevin in England, have been extremely generous with their considerable knowledge and enthusiasm, as well as giving me so much of their valuable time. I should like to thank them from the bottom of my heart for their help and support. Thank you also for your time and interest in my story.

Best Wishes, and Happy Beanie Hunting!

Duncan Willis

✒ ✒ ✒ ✒ ✒

I would like to thank Duncan for sharing this fascinating story with us. I have to admit I was a little skeptical at first, and I expressed this to Duncan. He graciously relieved my mind and gave me the proof I needed to write this article. He even called me from the UK and we spoke for over 35 minutes.

To sum up his Beanie Prototype find would be simply to say "SOME MEN HAVE ALL THE LUCK!!!!"

✐ ✐ ✐ ✐ ✐

UPDATE: Prototype Beanie, 8-3-97

This particular story received so much attention that I decided to ad closure by updating it. The bidding auction which was displayed on the Lemon Lainey site was a huge success. There was a total of thirty eight bids placed, many by the same individuals.

The starting bid price was $500.00 The final bid was placed on 7-30-97 in the amount of $1,400.00!!!

Has being the owner of this Prototype Bunny changed your life in any way?

Yes, it has, quite dramatically. I include Prototype Floppity in the whole Internet/computer phenomenon so far as my family is concerned, because we only bought our first 'proper' computer in January of this year, and it has had a tremendous impact on our lives. We only discovered Beanies by chance as a result of correspondence with an Internet friend in Texas, and we have now spent many happy hours hunting for those elusive little fellows. We have made friends with many Americans and, of course, Elaine and Kevin of Lemon Lainey Design here in England, all purely through having a computer, and through that, getting hooked on Beanies.

Did the auction run as smoothly as anticipated?

Never having had personal experience of an auction of any kind before, I really didn't know what to expect. However, I have to say that I thought it all went very smoothly. Credit for this must surely go to Kevin and Elaine, for without whose tremendous skills, patience and knowledge of Beanies, the auction would never have happened at all.

Once the prototype was posted for viewing on the Lemon Lainey site, did you ever have a problem with any individuals not believing in it's existence?

We had, I believe, two people who said they thought that Prototype Floppity was a fake. This I can perfectly understand because nowhere on the Bunny was there any reference to Ty, and with an increasing number of fakes and "altered" Beanies on the market, I expected people to be a bit skeptical.

However, I can assure you that Prototype Floppity is absolutely genuine, and my conversations with Patricia Roache at Ty, UK have confirmed that to my satisfaction. I would never have offered him for sale, had there been even a shadow of doubt in my mind that he wasn't the real thing.

Can you share any information about the individual who now owns the Prototype?

Only that she is a VERY serious collector who lives in Kentucky. I know that Prototype Floppity has gone to a good home and will be well looked after and appreciated by someone who knows exactly how special he really is. We have already had e-mails from people offering significantly more money for him than Prototype Floppity earned at auction ($1,400). We have passed these messages on to his new owner, but I very much doubt that she will sell him.

Photo credit: Elaine Smith
Lemon Lainey Design

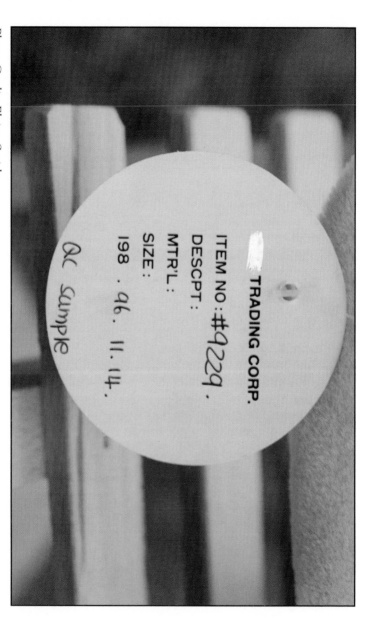

Now that the Prototype Floppity has been sold and has a new home, how do you feel about having to part with him?

Sad, of course. It has been great fun finding, researching, and finally auctioning such a unique Beanie. We'll never see another Beanie quite so rare as Prototype Floppity—he really was a once-in-a-lifetime find. I'll really miss my regular checks on the auction page to see how the bids are going. Unfortunately, once we had identified Floppity's background and realized that he might be worth a lot of money, it was inevitable that we would have to sell him—we simply could not justify keeping such a valuable item purely for the sake of interest. This has been made even more important in the last few days as I have now lost the job I love, and have been doing for the last seven years, and we really do need every penny to pay the mortgage and support our two young children.

Would you please list the Beanies which you have in your collection which are for sale. Would you include their prices and explain what makes them so special. Also please include where individuals may inquire about your Beanies.

We have bought additional stocks of a number of rare and retired Beanies, and sell them via Lemon Lainey's Website in her Beanie Mall section. You can access Duncan's On-Line Beanie Shop directly through the following address.
http://www.lemonlaineydesign.com/mall/duncan/beanieshop.html
Currently we have on offer Rex ($220); Bumble ($200); Caw ($200); Bubbles ($40); Kiwi ($60); Mystic Fine Hair ($90) and Radar ($50) amongst others.

My thanks to everyone who took part in the auction, and all to those Beanie collectors who visited the site—we hope that you had fun, and perhaps one day you will find a rare, or even a unique Beanie Prototype yourself, just like I did!! I very much hope that you do. That's part of the fun of Beanie Hunting—you just might turn up something really interesting, but even if you don't, you still have one of the most adorable soft toys ever. (My four year old daughter, Pippa, is curled up asleep in her bed with Bessie the Cow cuddled in the crook of her arm— what more could anyone ask of a soft toy than that it brings such pleasure and comfort to a child?)

Best wishes,

Duncan

After conducting Duncan's interview I couldn't help getting a little choked up. This man is truly one in a million. I believe that there is a plan and a purpose for every aspect of life. This man's rare find has served a very valuable purpose.

Not only was Duncan fortunate enough to find this Prototype, but he also realized that it belonged to a true Beanie collector.

CHAPTER TWELVE

Ms. Janie Teaches Beanie Classes

This article is about Beanie Babie classes I taught after being approached by a teacher who had taught my daughter last year. She knew of my interest in Beanie Babies and had seen the newspaper article that "Potomac News" had done on me, and wanted to know if I would be interested in doing a Beanie Babie class for her students. I encourage any school volunteers, moms, dads and anyone who may have some free time to use the information in this article and share it with the children in your school district. The children, as well as the teachers, would certainly be grateful, for a short break.

Ms. Janie Teaches Beanie Classes

After the "Potomac News" article came out, I was suddenly very popular and called the "Beanie Lady" by most kids at school. One day Mrs. Spears, a former teacher, who had taught my daughter, approached me wanting to know if I would be interested in talking with her class about Beanie

Babies. She stated that the children had been exceptionally good all year and had worked hard, and she wanted to reward them with a special treat.

Although I was excited about the prospect of teaching a Beanie Babie class, I was also a little frightened. I had never attempted anything along these lines before. "What would I say? How would I keep their attention?"

As the day grew closer, I became more anxious. I prepared a hand out which gave the site location where my articles could be read and also provided information about the club with which I was working. I scanned some pictures of my own posed Beanie Babies on the flyer to make it more attractive, and also listed the titles of each article.

Finally the big day came. I left for school early. Unfortunately my daughter left her musical instrument at home and needed it delivered to her. While I was waiting for my class to start I was approached by Mrs. Harris, 1st grade teacher at Henderson Elementary School in Virginia. She started talking about Beanie Babies and I explained to her that I was giving a Beanie Babie class for Mrs. Spears. Mrs. Harris asked what time the class started. Since I told her I had about 25 to 30 minutes before I was due, she asked if I would mind visiting her class and sharing my knowledge with her students in the interim. I agreed.

The children in Mrs. Harris class recognized me from the newspaper article. Mrs. Harris introduced me and asked the class to please raise their hands if they had questions. I explained how I got started collecting Beanie Babies and showed them the retired pieces I had collected over the last six months. I asked the children questions about Beanies in order to find out just how much they knew. Much to my surprise I found they knew quite a bit. I shared some valuable information with them and thanked them for inviting me into their classroom.

Before I knew it my time was up. Mrs. Spears' class was expecting me and I had to go. The children made it difficult, it was obvious that they wanted to hear more. So I told them I would give Mrs. Harris some information for her to pass along to them. The children were extremely attentive and very courteous. I really enjoyed sharing information with such well-behaved students. I commend Mrs. Harris and her teacher's aid for a job well done.

When I finally made it to Mrs. Spears' class, she was anxiously awaiting my arrival. She told me that the kids were very excited and had brought in their own Beanies from home to share with me. I explained how I started collecting Beanie Babies and how I had my own set. I explained how I used the Internet to do research and gather most of my material. I also talked to them about the advantages of the Secondary Market and warned them about the disadvantages. I encouraged them to play with their Beanies and I told them that, unless they wanted to be serious collectors, they should enjoy them while they were young.

Of course, I did explain the collecting end of it as well. I reminded them that if they wanted to play with and collect Beanies, they should remove the ear tags and put them in a safe place. This way, if they ever did decide to fall in line with other collectors, their Beanies would still have perfect ear tags. I told the children that not only do I collect Beanie Babies, but I also enclose my personal set in a Zip Lock bag to keep them from fading and getting dusty.

I passed out the handouts and they all seemed to enjoy it very much, especially the pictures.

Next I dug into my bag of goodies and showed what I had. I began off by explaining what to look for in manufacturing mistakes. Dottie, with a Sparky tag, and Bongo, with the wrong tail color were my examples. None of the kids were aware of these mistakes and could not wait to go home to see whether they had any mistakes in their collection.

By this point I could tell that I had the children's full attention, as they anticipated my every move. Next I started pulling out some of my retired collection. The children were getting more excited by the minute. I showed the whole 1997 retired collection to date and shared a Bumble the Bee from the 1996 retired collection. Garcia and Bumble were the children's favorite until I brought out Maple. They went crazy! They had never seen Maple, and some of the children had never even heard of him.

I tried to answer all of the children's questions to the best of my ability. Most of the questions asked were regarding the dollar amount of certain Beanies. The number one question was, "Where can we find more Beanie Babies?" I had anticipated this question, so I was prepared to answer. I gave the children names of the stores which carry Beanies in our area. I also shared some information about a contest that I would be sponsoring with the Beanie Babies Buddies Club. I encouraged them to use the Internet in a positive way and on those hot summer days, to go searching the world for their Beanie Babies. It was difficult to leave this fine group of students; they were so well behaved and were grateful to me for being there.

That day, when my daughter returned home from school, she informed me she had something to give me from Mrs. Spears' class. The children had drawn their favorite Beanie Babie and written a thank you note to include with their drawing. Not only was I extremely touched, but I was also very proud to have been able to share my knowledge with Mrs. Harris' and Mrs. Spears' classes.

Here is a sample of some of the notes I got from Mrs. Spears' class. These notes will be put right next to my Beanie Memorabilia and will be cherished for many years. I love all of the notes and wish I could share each and every one, but that is simply not possible.

Dear Mrs. Daniels,
Thank you sooo much for sharing your Beanie Baby wisdom with us. One thing is for sure, I'm not letting my Digger or Derby out of my sight and the next time

I visit my aunt in Canada I'm going to get Maple.
Thank you so much, I really appreciate it. (Latoya)

Dear Mrs. Daniels,
Thank you for coming to our class. I really learned a
lot about Beanie Babies. My favorite fact was about
Bongo's tail. I was really surprised about how much
stuff you knew about Beanie Babies. Once again I
thank you. (Andy)

Dear Mrs. Daniels,
Thank you so much for coming into our class to talk
about Beanie Babies. I really enjoyed it. I'm glad you
told us where to get Beanie Babies. I can't find them
anywhere. I also liked looking at your Beanie Babies.
Thanks again. (Ellen)

Dear Mrs. Daniels,
Thank you for coming to our class and telling us more
about Beanie Babies. I really enjoyed seeing all your
Beanie Babies and seeing your pictures that you took.
I really wish that you could have stayed for a longer
time. (Jennifer)

Dear Mrs. Daniels,
I really thank you for coming and showing us some of
your Beanie Babies. Thank you for telling me that I
should always ask my parents before sending money
on line. I know you like Garcia. I do too. (Caitlyn)

I was contacted by Mrs. Massie, another teacher from
Henderson. She wanted to know if I would be interested in
conducting a Beanie Babies class for her students. I conducted the class just as I had done for Mrs. Spears and the
children were very excited. I wasn't sure if it was because of
Beanie Babies or because it was the last full day of school.

There is one difference in this story compared to the other stories. When I brought out Maple, Mrs. Massie had her camera ready to go. She took a few pictures and seemed just as excited as the children were. She also was the only teacher that I noticed that took notes about where to find Beanie Babies!

I have to honestly say that I really enjoyed this experience. It was my pleasure to be able to put smiles on so many faces.

CHAPTER THIRTEEN

Let's Have a Beanie Party

Hey, it's that time of year again. One in which, when you become an adult, you hate the sound of but, when you're a kid, it's the best day in the world.

It's a Birthday Party!

But wait…there are no Beanie party supplies on the market. What has happened? There are Beanie accessories all over the Internet and in the stores, but no Beanie party supplies.

This article will show you how to have a fun Beanie party without the frills of Beanie faces all over your plate.

It has always fascinated me that with all of the Beanie copycats and all of the Beanie accessories, that someone hasn't come up with Beanie party supplies. It is a known fact that the Ty Company is extremely busy these days. They are opening up more and more warehouses. They are signing on new accounts every day. They are doing everything a successful company should do in order to maintain success except for one thing: THEY AREN'T MAKING BEANIE BABIES FAST ENOUGH!!!

Not only is there a shortage of supplies of these little darlings, which have taken over most of our lives, but there are no party supplies! I have had several collectors contact me asking for suggestions for Beanie parties. If Ty won't design a party package for Beanie Babies, why not design your own? Next, you will find a few suggestions which may be of some help.

Invitations

There are a couple of things you can do:

✍ You can take a roll of film and photograph a bunch of Beanies, or just your favorite Beanie. After you have the roll developed, take the pictures and glue them onto a card. On the inside of the card you may want to supply the Beanies' names and poems. Add the details of the party.

✍ Another idea is to look for a Beanie with your same birthdate or month that you do. Use the Beanie's picture on the front of the card for your decoration. On the inside of the card you can include additional information if you wish or simply just include details of the party.

✍ Take a picture with your child holding their favorite Beanie. Take it and scan it into a computer and incorporate the text as you wish.

Game Ideas

Beanie Bag Game:

Put a few different Beanies in a bag—have the child close their eyes and reach into the bag. Ask them to feel around and identify one of the Beanies and then pull it out and go on to the next child.

You also can ask the children to draw and color their own Beanie. After they have finished, ask them to date it and name it; they also may want to include their own poem.

Puzzle Beanie:
Take some photographs of Beanies and enlarge them. Cut them in different angles and ask the children to paste them back together.

Guess That Beanie:
Give the children the names of four Beanies. Tell them that you will draw portions of one of the Beanies. See how long it takes for them to guess the right one.

Name That Beanie:
One by one have the children describe their favorite Beanie without disclosing its name. Have the other children identify it.

Beanie Shards:
Put Beanies names into a paper bag. Have the children reach in the bag and pull out a Beanie name. They have to act like the animal whose name they have drawn until the other children figure it out.

Beanie Word Search Games:
Everybody loves a good word search. Why not make one up yourself? If you need help, find examples of searches I have made in Chapter 22.

Beanie Scramble Word Game:
Take the names of Beanies and scramble them— Example: ARGICA; Answer: Garcia

Beanie Food: How Brave Are You????

Make some Jello and let the children cut out designs using cookie cutters to represent their favorite Beanie.

Mix a batch of cookie dough. Use a recipe that can be handled easily and which is not sticky. Ask the children to sculpt their favorite Beanie. Bake the Beanies and then allow the children to decorate them. It would be a good idea to have a few different colors of icing as well as an assortment of sprinkles available. Pillsbury Cookie Dough in the freezer section of your grocery store works well for this project. Make sure to have the kids sprinkle a little flour on their hands to keep the dough from sticking. Let's face it…if it isn't messy, it isn't fun!

Beanie Crafts

Let's Make Beanie Stickers:

Go to any paper product store and purchase sticker paper. Let the kids draw and color their own Beanies. Once they have finished cut them out and let them wear them proudly on their clothing.

Make Your Own Beanie Collars:

Purchase some ribbon, beads with letters on them, stickers, fake gems and Velcro. Let the kids cut a piece of ribbon to fit their favorite Beanie. Help them super glue a piece of Velcro at each end to attach to their Beanie after they have decorated it.

Beanie Canvas Pictures:

Take a photograph of a Beanie and glue it onto a piece of canvas. Make sure that there is at least 1" border of the canvas showing after the picture is glued. Have the kids sew around their picture using a light weight yarn for a framed effect. You may have to purchase large needles made for yarn. This project is not for kids under the age of 10.

Grand Finale

Goodie Bags always seem to be a problem. We always seem to spend too much money, especially when it comes to older kids. They cannot be satisfied with plastic whistles and fake money. The perfect solution would be to come up with an idea that would cost around $5.00 a child or less. For example, fill a heart shaped piñata with candy and small envelopes. Inside each envelope put the name of a Beanie. After the piñata is broken and each child has an envelope, present them with the Beanie whose name was in their envelope. It sure beats buying tons of questionable goodies.

Visit the Ty site at www.ty.com; this site has a lot of kids' games that can be copied and used for your party. Copy their calendar of the month and let the children color it for use as a placemat. Other sites that also contain games for children are The Beanie Babies Buddies Club and BeanieMom.

With a little thought and planning your child's party can easily be turned into something memorable. Not only are the projects a lot of fun, but it also helps to involve your child with their own party.

CHAPTER FOURTEEN

Beanie Accessories

Beanie Babies were selling like hot cakes whenever they could be found. The second hottest-selling items were Beanie Babies accessories. Not only were items from Beanie clothes to furniture being designed, but most were reasonably priced.

Beanie Accessories—
What Will They Think of Next?

It was getting to the point that you could not go anywhere without hearing about or seeing Beanie accessories. There was a wide range of variety, and most of them were cleverly designed. Because these items were selling as quickly as the Beanie Babies themselves, it was time to do some investigating: "Which items were the most popular, which were the most practical, and what were the price range for these accessories?" These were the questions I wanted answered. The Internet came in handy. It helped answer all of these questions and more.

There were tons of Beanie Collars for sale. Some were very colorful, some had names, some fastened with Velcro, and others hooked on. Prices ranged from $1 to $5. There was also a large variety of leashes, the two most popular having stationary or swivel hardware attached to the collars. Prices ranged from $2 to $7. Beanie Tote bags could also be found. My favorite one had the word "Beanies" machine-stitched on the bag. It was of very good quality.

The Teenie Beanies were not left out. There was a bag designed for them as well. Prices varied because of the large selection and how much you wanted added to it. I found that these particular bags from Nancy were the best available. I've even bought a few myself. Her e-mail address is Nancybus@ aol.com. She is currently designing a Christmas line, which I understand is to die for. This woman told me that her machine could do everything but cook dinner!

The most practical accessory award went to the Beanie Tag Protector. This clever invention keeps tags from bending and tearing. You could purchase 50 for $10; another style was offered for 50 for $7.

The most popular accessory award goes to Piggybacks by Mara. This well thought out accessory allows you to tote your Teenie Beanies along for the ride. They really are adorable. The price is around $3.

Three different style tee shirts could also be found on the market. Two of them were designed with Beanie look-likes, and the third appeared to be copied right from Ty's Beanie Babies pictures. Prices ranged from $9.99 and $14.99 for kids, and adults' ranged from $15.99 and up.

Buttons were another very popular item. I have purchased buttons from PJ. And found them to be of good quality and would purchase again if need be. Prices range from $1 to $1.75 each depending on quantity.

It would simply be impossible to list or write about all of the Beanie Babie accessories which have hit the market. Here is a partial list without descriptions of a few more I found on the Internet :

Beanie Friends in the Wild. Nuts, Baldy, Kiwi, Congo and Bongo.

Lizzy

- Beanie Trading Cards
- Beanie Houses
- Beanie Posters
- Beanie Jewelry
- Beanie Sun Glasses
- Beanie Adults' and Children's Hats
- Beanie Clothes
- Beanie Bumper Stickers
- Beanie Bins
- Beanie Checkbook Covers
- Beanie Beds, Hammocks, Cradles, Benches
- Bean Pole Display
- Beanie Bunks

While doing this research a few sites were contacted and given the opportunity to advertise their Beanie accessories in their own words.

✒   ✒   ✒   ✒   ✒

My name is PJ and this is a home based business. My accessories are: "Beanie Buttons." They are 2-3/4" Round Buttons. Currently, I offer a choice of 15 different sayings, and six different color choices for the background. They can be worn on T-shirts, hats, purses, bookbags or just anywhere!
Prices: 1/$1.75, 3/$5.00, 5/$7.50, 10/$12.50, 15+/$1.00 each. (plus shipping)
I also offer group, club, school and church organization discounts, large quantity discounts, and wholesale prices.
My web site is...
http://members.tripod.com/~pjs/index.htm
I accept personal check or money orders. (No credit cards, because I am keeping the cost of the buttons down!)

The order can be placed by sending payment along with order to:
PJ Creations
PO Box 596
Dyer, IN 46311
Orders are shipped within two-three days from receipt of payment. I am a reputable seller, and I can produce references!
Hope to hear from you soon!
Thank you! PJ

✎ ✎ ✎ ✎ ✎

From: HALG1345@aol.com
The G Group Marketing of Northbrook, Ill
I have published a 52-page diary and note books for Beanie Babies collectors, this book includes a complete inventory system to help you keep track of your Beanie collection; it has a numerical listing of all current and retired Beanie Babies with names, birthdays and other information. There is a section to keep telephone numbers, and e-mail addresses of other collectors in. It also has a diary to keep notes on your Babies and other important notes in. Published on June 1, 1997 we have shipped over 10,000 books the first month. The retail price is $5.00 each and can be viewed on site htp://www.catalog.com/beanies/diary. The book can be found in retail stores nationally or can be ordered through our web site. We are also looking for dealers to sell this book. Thank you for your interest.

✎ ✎ ✎ ✎ ✎

From: "Jeffry Freiburger" <jeffry@execpc.com>
Hi:

My name is Jodie Freiburger and I sell Cuddle Bags for Beanies. Cuddle Bags are hand made. I choose material from the local fabric stores that matches Beanies or certain animals. I currently have over 35 styles of Cuddle Bags. Each Cuddle Bag is fur-lined and comes with a matching pillow. Cuddle Bags are $7 each, or less if you buy in quantity.

My website address is http://www.execpc.com/~jeffry/cuddle.htm.

Cuddle Bags have been selling great over the Internet and I have also done some local craft shows.

Jodie Freiburger

✍ ✍ ✍ ✍ ✍

"Piggybacks by Mara" are an accessory idea that came out of the Teenie Beanie craze. I thought it would be fun to be able to attach baby teenies to their Beanie parent like a baby carrier. It makes it look like the Teenies are getting a piggyback ride. The Teenies little feet stick out of the holes cut in the bottom of the carrier, just like a "real" baby carrier. "Piggybacks by Mara" can also be worn on the child's wrist. Put the Teenie inside and strap it on bracelet-style. I'm from Bloomington, MN near the Mall of America, so many stores there and in the Minneapolis and St. Paul area have bought "Piggybacks" to sell. Over the Internet I've gotten some business too. I also go to Beanie swaps and art fairs. Altogether I've sold over 1500. They are cute, inexpensive, and popular. They are made in several bright colors of backpack nylon with colored "Velcro-type" straps. They sell for $3 apiece. Wholesale prices available for stores or people buying more than 1 dozen.

Please visit my website for a look www.isd.net/plewando

Thank you, Mara Lewandowski

✒ ✒ ✒ ✒ ✒

Name: Kathy Gray (CasinoBuni@aol.com)
The name-meaning prints aren't actually "used" with the Beanie Babies. They are frameable printouts on graphic backgrounds that contain information on the meaning of the name.
Beanie Babie Name Meanings—Includes name meaning, personality traits, birthdate (optional) and other information based on the name.
$7.00 (includes shipping)
Off-line selling has been great, I've had a few orders through the web site. Web address: http://members. aol.com/casinobuni

✒ ✒ ✒ ✒ ✒

My name is Beth Formby. The Beanie collars are made in three different patterns of material and they connect with Velcro. They sell for 1.50 each. The collars have done well and are listed and the materials shown, on the web page www.petdecos.com.

✒ ✒ ✒ ✒ ✒

Dear Ms. Janie,
I would be pleased if you included information about my site in your article. My name is Pam Gaborski and I design and make wooden accessories for all bean-bag stuffed animals. I currently sell hammocks, beds, cradles and benches. Each item is carefully hand crafted of fine American hardwoods and high quality fabric. The beds and craddles include a blanket and pillow, and the benches include a cushion. The prices are:

Cradle	$9
Bed	$14

Bench $14
Hammock $13

Plus shipping.

Not only have these accessories been a popular product, but I have enjoyed designing and building them. I personally believe they extend the collecting of Beanies to a creative play activity.

The address for Pam's Beanie Stuffed Animal Accessories is: www.frontiernet.net/~gaborski

Pam Gaborski

❧ ❧ ❧ ❧ ❧

Before long, hopefully we will see Beanie party supplies, Beanie food items, Beanie diapers, Beanie bottles, and a Beanie clothing line for children. Don't forget the adults, they love Beanies too!! And, if we are all lucky, we may even see Teenie Beanies again (someday).

CHAPTER FIFTEEN

This Madness Has Got to Stop!!!

The Beanie Babie madness is like a bad cold that keeps lingering.

Beanie Babie stories used to contain information about how cute and reasonably priced they were. Now all we hear about are fights, mob scenes, and long lines.

This Madness Has Got to Stop!!!

Although Beanies still remain very popular, many kids and adults are getting tired of the madness that goes along with collecting them.

- Ty has had problems producing Beanie Babies.
- Store are limited to the amount they can order.
- More and more people are collectng Beanie Babies, secondary market is involved.

In most cases, $5.00 for a Beanie is a thing of the past.

Many store owners do not agree with Ty's policies and would like to see them changed but will continue to sell Beanie Babies because, according to them, it's quick cash.

The Beanie Babies are such hot sellers that the store gener-
ates a quick cash flow whenever they arrive.

It's almost like a love-hate relationship!!!

While new accounts are being opened daily, it also means
more limits being put on the product. Just about every store I
know that used to ship Beanie Babies can no longer do so.
They simply do not get enough stock to satisfy their local customers, much less their out-of-state customers.

New accounts are also aware of this popularity and have
imposed a limit of two to six Beanie Babies per customer.
Except for Nordstroms, of course. They probably receive
more than 20 small shops put together. I have heard that
they, too, have imposed a limit. I would venture to say it is
somewhere between four or six of each kind. That's not bad
if you happen to be lucky enough to get 20,000 in and at least
40 to 50 different styles at one time.

A situation was occurring with a new account which
sounded kind of strange. This individual has sold Ty plush for
over 15 years. He had just ordered Beanie Babies, and, after
his first shipment arrived, he learned how popular they were.
He decided to make this work to his advantage by telling the
customer that he did not have any Beanie Babies in stock. He
did not offer to accept a wish list from them, but he did offer
to put their name on a telephone list. He claimed that once
his shipment came in he would contact them.

I entered my name on the list. Fifteen minutes after I
arrived home the phone rang and it was the store owner. He
said he had just gotten his shipment in. The kids and I
packed up and away we went. However, when we got back to
this store, we found that I was only allowed to purchase whatever was in the bag with my phone number on it. There were
four Beanies in the bag. I could purchase all four or take any
one of the four. I was not allowed to purchase any more than
four, nor was I allowed to switch them for others that I might
need. After I experienced this, I shared the news with a
friend of mine. I asked her to go to this store and see if the

same thing would happen to her. I wasn't surprised the next day when she told me that the exact same thing had happened to her as well.

This store owner knew that he had something half the world wanted. He was using this product to get people into his store more often. He didn't care if you purchased them or not, because he knew that someone else would. At the same time he would show you other merchandise (some Beanie related) in order to make a sale. Some people might consider this to be a very good business approach, but I was definitely turned off by it. He knew that there were only five locations which sold Beanie Babies locally. As far as he was concerned, he was Mohammed sitting on top of the world. If there *was* a world called Greedsville! (In my opinion many store owners should visit it, because that's where they belong!!!)

There have also been several stories about how many stores are now charging inflated prices. This has been reported over and over. New releases are selling for $10 to $20 a-piece on the Internet as well as in stores.

While visiting a mall, Beanies were not only discovered, but they were actually in stock. However, there was a sign posted, "You have to purchase $10 of our store merchandise before you can purchase one Beanie Babie." I informed the store clerk that this was against Ty's policy, and that they could not do this. I also told him that I would be reporting him. He informed me that he was not the only store operating under these terms. Needless to say, I did not purchase anything, and, once again, I came up empty handed.

What does all of this mean to the average collector?

It actually could mean a few things. If you started collecting Beanie Babies in the last two months, it may very well take you a long time before your set is completed. It also appears to me that, if collectors choose to continue collecting, that they may have to resort to the secondary market with its higher prices. Our only option is to do what we have been doing already—stand in long lines only to end up with one or two Beanie Babies or possibly go home empty handed.

I have witnessed others setting up tables on their front lawns and selling Beanie Babies. One women must of have had over 300 for sale. She even had a police officer guarding her stash! It won't be long before we find Beanie Babies being sold in the strangest places.

Imagine this!!

You stop at a public restroom to freshen up. As you enter the restroom, much to your surprise, there is a cart full of Beanie Babies waiting to be bought.

Sounds far-fetched doesn't it? NOT REALLY!!! If I've learned anything, it is that people will stop at nothing to buy or sell Beanie Babies. There have been many reports about fights breaking out, children's strollers being knocked over, stores being ransacked and even Ty's own employees stealing Beanie Babies.

In my opinion, one or two things has happened. Either there is something in the pellets of these Beanie Babies that make people act this way, or we simply have lost our minds. Who knows!! But this madness has to stop before someone gets seriously hurt!

Ty made these Beanie Babies for kids to collect safely. If we all can remember the purpose of this fad, kids would be safer and happier.

CHAPTER SIXTEEN

Beanie Swap-N-Meet

These meets have become so popular that it's almost impossible to keep up with them. Individuals, tired of waiting for Ty to produce their product, have taken matters into their own hands. Beanie swap meets are cropping up all over the nation faster than weeds.

On June 21, 1997 there was a Beanie Swap meet in Dale City, VA which was held at the VFW on Minnieville Road. I had the opportunity to speak briefly with Sherry, the organizer of this meet, via telephone. After gathering what little information I got, I decided to check around and see whether anyone was planning to attend this meet. I needed more information, but I had to finish up articles I'd already started and simply could not go, myself. I was able to gather some valuable information from trusted, reliable sources who reported the following:

- The Beanie Swap meet started at 9 AM and ended at 5 PM. From what I understand it was a huge success.

✐ Steady crowds streamed in all day long at a cost of $5.00 for adults and free for children 12 & under.

✐ The venders' tables were $20.00 for half of table and $40.00 a whole table. There were approximately 75 to 100 venders.

Some of the more popular items sold were:

Pastel Bunnies at $20.00 each.

Maple sold for $75.00 and up.

Dinosaurs went for $250.00

Current Beanies, with the exception of Spooky and a few others, went for between $10.00 and $15.00

There was a full basket of the retired January Beanies selling for $600.00

My friend, Debbie who attended the meet, was there to finish her daughter's collection. She traded three current Beanies for Radar, three new Beanies for Spooky, and one Valentino for Tamagotchi.

On July 13, 1997 there was another Beanie Swap Meet in Tyson's Corner, VA at the Holiday Inn. Kristy, another very good trusted reliable source, reported the following:

✐ Admittance cost was $5.00 for adults and free for children 12 and under.

✐ 13 Dealers attended this event with some of them renting two or three tables at $50.00 each.

✐ Between the hours of 1 PM and 3 PM the crowd was estimated to be around 30 to 40 people.

✐ The most popular current Beanie Babies, with the exception of the new releases, were Inky, Spooky, Valentino, Mystic and Magic.

✐ Current Beanies averaged $10.00 to $15.00 with some going for $20.00.

✐ The new Mother's Day releases were being sold for

$15.00 to $30.00.
- ✧ Maple's went for as much as $100.00 to $200.00.
- ✧ Teenie Beanies also made a guest appearance and were selling for $6.00 to $10.00. There were a lot of Snorts, Goldies and Speedies to be had.
- ✧ Some of the prices at this swap meet were:
  Flash and Splash sold for $50.00 each
  Digger sold for $35.00 each
  Sparky and Grunt sold for $75.00 each
  Bubbles sold for $45.00 each
  Garcia sold for $75.00 to $100.00 each
  Radar sold for $45.00 to $75.00 each, depending on the vendor.
  Chops sold for $80.00 each
  Sting sold for $75.00 each
  Cranberry Teddy sold for $325.00 each
  Web the spider sold for $200.00 each
  Steg sold for $300.00 to $350.00 each
  Old Patti with tags sold for $300.00 each
- ✧ New current releases were selling hotter than the retired ones!!!

These organized meets are not only a lot of fun, but also seem like the only way any of us will be able to obtain Beanies these days. In my opinion, it won't be long before we see Ty Warner organizing a Beanie Swap meet of his own. "Hey, wait a minute, maybe that's where all the Beanies will show up!!!"

This just goes to show you, nothing will stop a Beanie collectors on a mission. They can smell those Beanies a mile away. And they will travel even further just to get their hands on them. "Can you blame them, these Beanies are hotter than the summer sun."

CHAPTER SEVENTEEN

Beanies by the Sea

The Beanie explosion seemed to be slowing down.

Leads were not being generated as often and the lack of Beanie Supply was forcing people to talk about new subjects.

During this dry spell there was a vacation with my name written all over it.

It was time for me to soak up some sun and put Beanies to rest for a while. The family and I traveled to sunny Ocean City, Maryland. The weather was hot and muggy, but the breeze from the ocean was refreshing.

After coming in from the beach one day, I decided to check out the local publications for dining and entertainment places.

While flipping through an Ocean City Visitors' Guide, I spotted a page with Beanies on it.

My first thought was, "Oh no, they found me!"

My second thought was, "Did I really want to spend my vacation looking and talking about Beanies?" *Needless to say my second thought won!!*

I proceeded to instruct my family to get dressed and explained where we were headed. Hubby was not over excited, but the children were elated. They were hoping to find some of the new releases which they needed for their collection.

We arrived at the Candy Kitchen on 23rd Street. As we spied every inch of the store, the only Beanie we spotted was Zip, the black cat. We were told that he was all that remained. I ask for directions to other Candy Kitchen locations and asked if they knew if any Beanies were available. I was told to go to 53rd Street.

As we approached 53rd Street, we noticed a large sign outside the establishment announcing that they had Beanies. Believe it or not, even Hubby got excited. The children and I ran into the store and discovered we had hit the jack pot. There were Beanies in baskets everywhere.

The going price for most current pieces was $6.99. I noticed Spooky, Magic and Valentino displayed behind the counter. I asked their prices and was told the following:

Because they are so rare and are up for retirement they would cost more.

I agreed that they are hard to find, but no store should speculate about the retirement of any Beanies for sale until the actual retirement date is announced. I voiced my opinion, which was to no avail. I then learned, in order to purchase these Beanies, you would have to buy a package deal.

This deal contained one hard to find Beanie, one small bag of salt water taffy, one small bag of gummy bears, one plastic pail and one Beanie collar all for the price of $19.95 plus tax.

At first I thought that this was ridiculous, but then I remembered seeing Spooky and Valentino going for $40.00 to $60.00 on the Internet, and they didn't even offer any candy with the sale.

As I was contemplating whether or not to purchase one of these so called hard to find Beanies, I spotted Bubbles, the fish.

Beanies soaking up the sun, waiting for Ty, to make them new friends.

Pinches, Claude, Lizzy, Digger and Speedy.

Once again I inquired. I was told that Bubbles came with the same package deal but would cost $29.95. In this case I felt that the price was a little high. Even though Bubbles was retired, the going price was somewhere around $25.00. "But then it dawned on me." Where could you go and purchase gummy bears, salt water taffy, a plastic pail and a Beanie collar for $4.95???

"Looks like it was a good deal after all."

Other places that carried Beanies were the Kite Loft on the boardwalk. Although they only had Doddle, the rooster, they did carry Beanies and sold them for $9.99 each.

I also ventured into a store called Plaza Beach Sundries on 28th Street. The owner and I engaged into a long conversation about the Ty Company and Beanies. She expressed her disappointment about Ty and their inability to produce their products. She also explained why she no longer puts the Beanies out for display. If she notices a mother and child wondering around the stuffed animals, she ask them if they are interested in Beanies, That is when she "has" them. She has been angered by individuals patronizing her store and buying up all of the Beanies just to sell them for higher prices. She wants to make sure that, in her opinion, they get sold to the "rightful buyers—the kids."

I still can't help but wonder, what it is about these Beanies that keep attracting me? I would think that it would have weakened by now.

But I have learned one thing, "It just won't go away.

To be honest, I'm not sure I want it too."

CHAPTER EIGHTEEN

The Beanie Babies Buddies Club Speaks Out!

Featuring Randy & Sandy Jones

While I've enjoyed the pleasure of working with the Beanie Master (Randy Jones) he has often expressed his feelings and concerns regarding Beanie Babies.

Because of his outspokenness, it was time to allow him to voice his opinion in his own words.

Please bear in mind that this individual truly enjoys operating his Beanie site and loves kids even more.

The Beanie Master Speaks Out!!!

How has your life changed since you got involved with Beanie Babies?

I USED to think I spent a lot of time on the computer...then along came Beanies and the BBB Club. Now, I spend the bulk of my free time on Beanie related material. Just answering e-mail and updating the pages consumes a lot of time. As for trying to go looking around the net for what's new...danged near never get time to do that! The family has gotten used to me glued to this keyboard and monitor, trying to finish "one more thing" before we can eat dinner or head to the pool.

Of course, that's just the tip of the iceberg. With all the world-wide international acclaim I receive daily as the BeanieMaster, the talk shows, the book deals, the movie rights and all the calls we get from the White House to come on down and bring our Beanies, well, I guess you might say, time is at a premium. Still, I wouldn't change a thing...except for a $10 bill to buy a new Beanie!

How hard is it for you to obtain your own Beanie Babies?

Next to impossible. We hunted them from Pennsylvania to South Carolina and only found ONE. We keep hitting the local stores, only to find out that we're two hours too late. It's going to take FOREVER to find those new May releases!<Grin> We're really thankful we managed to get a collection together just WEEKS before the Great Collapse of '97. Ahhhh, was that a terrible time, and little did we know how long it would continue. Trying to put together a set now would be a real problem. Still, we give it our best family shot and try to get lucky with a new one whenever possible.

On a popularity scale of one to ten, ten being the highest, where do you think Beanies would range?

In this household, 10. I have no idea how the rest of the world would judge them. It seems that as I talk to folks, either they are totally aware of everything Beanie-related, or they look at me like I'm talking a foreign language. There don't seem to be many folks in the middle ground. Either you love 'em, or you don't know what they are!

Many people have had the opportunity to voice their opinion on the Secondary Market. How do you feel about this market and would you ever purchase from it?

Ha! I KNEW somebody would ask me about this one day. I'd buy a retired Beanie off the Market any time, if I were looking for one. As a rule, that's the only place you can find them, and it's a great use for the net. The activity level of trading and selling in our Club Forum never ceases to amaze me…and we're just a little bitty back-water club compared to some of the truly fine Beanie sites out there. As for the selling of current Beanies on the Secondary Market, well, it's like this:

I was, and still am, a little upset about the whole situation. It's extremely hard to find Beanies already, and to have individuals out there out there buying them up by the barrel-full to re-sell not only makes things even harder on the kids seeking them, but costs the kids more than it should to obtain Beanies. On the other hand, we're lucky enough to have a set, so all we're looking for is the new releases. That's a challenge, but not an insurmountable one. For folks that live too far from a Beanie outlet, or those needing just a few to complete their set, the Secondary Market can be a lifesaver. If you're willing to pay a little more for that needed Beanie, at least you have the ability to get it. I'm usually a little bit uneasy about exchanging money over the net, so I'd advise anybody doing so to try to make sure both sides are on the up and up.

The interesting thing is: all of this will be moot once TY gets their restructuring done, shipping gets back to normal, and that "Slow Boat From China" with all the goods picks up a little steam! Then we can all get back to the business at hand...Saturday Beanie hunting trips with the kids...something that used to be a family tradition.

What is your opinion about all of the Beanie accessories being created for sale; and, have you ever purchased any?

Oh yeah on this one! We have all kinds of accessories! We got the Beanie beds, folding beach chairs, collars, buttons, sleeping bags, and leashes. That's not to mention all the stuff my kids are constantly making on their own...necklaces, hats, and capes...the coolest of which are "Beanie Castles" made out of cardboard boxes. They decorate the inside with fabric and furniture made out of household items, cut windows and doors, slap 'em full of stickers...you name it. And it's a great place for all the accessories to be kept, instead of being scattered all over the house!

It seems like every day that I check mail, there's a new cool accessory site asking to be included on the Club site. Some of them are variations on a theme, but once in a while you get some great new ones that are still reasonably priced.

Which is your favorite Beanie and why?

Garcia, by far; always has been. He was named after Jerry Garcia of the Grateful Dead, and I weaned my teeth on that group way back in the "Good Old Days." Besides, I like the color mix, and he sits up very straight! I must have five of the little buggers sitting on my monitor, but they don't talk much. I like that in a pet.

What type of enjoyment or pleasure has operating your site given you?

> Well, it sure does keep me out of trouble. Instead of sitting in front of this silly toaster playing Doom2, I now try to keep things up to date. There's always a ton of e-mail, and some of it is a joy to answer.
>
> It's especially rewarding when a kid asks for some help on a page they're doing, and I'm able to point them in the right direction...then to see the results of kids that didn't have a clue about HTML a few weeks ago turn out a really fine page. THAT's what I call rewarding!
>
> The other thing we've enjoyed is keeping the site basically TEXT oriented. The site is intended for kids to pick up information and learn. We keep graphics to a minimum so things load as quickly as possible and you have to actually READ to learn anything. Education, and all that, eh. Not to many flashing signs, dancing monkeys or picture libraries—just plain old-fashioned reading. It's good for ya!

Many people would ask why an individual would dedicate so much time to operate a non-profit site. How would you answer that?

> Quite simple. I gave up trying to rationalize the whole thing, and for Christmas, my family got me a lobotomy. Since then everything has been, well, er, ahhh-hhhh...What was the question again?

If you were asked to sum up Beanie Babies in ten words or less. What would you say?

> Don't SAVE Beanies. Have FUN with them!
> (Hey...that's only nine words. I came in under the limit for a change!!!!! How'd that happen? You know,

at times I've been accused of rambling on, not making coherent statements, or even losing my train of thought all together. Thank Bob that didn't happen here. It's nice to be able to comply. And remember: Don't use big words when diminutives will suffice.)
NOVUS ORDO SECLORUM,
Randy Jones
Beanie Master, BBBC

Sandy Jones The Mistress of the Beanie Babie Buddies Club Speaks Out

I realized that Mrs. Jones was probably like most women. She held down a full time job, took care of her family and helped operate a Beanie Club. Her efforts could not go unrecognized.

Would you please provide a bio on yourself.

I have a degree in Elementary Education and Library Science. I have been teaching Kindergarten for almost 23 years. Randy and I have been married for 20 years. We have nine year old fraternal twin daughters, Heather and Laurel. And although Randy and I are the same age, he is MUCH older than I am.

How did the club begin?

It started in our living room then moved to the internet in October, 1996. It began as a club for kids up to 12 years old. When we started getting protesting messages from the teens and adults who found Beanies so adorable, we agreed that the club should be open to all ages.

I realize you work closely with the BeanieMaster. Could you please tell me what some of your duties are which involve operating the web site?

Mr. Randy Jones "Beanie Master"

Mrs. Sandy Jones

I have many duties but, luckily, I don't have to do them all on the same day! I help Heather, the President, answer her e-mail and look for answers to the members' questions. I edit the Beanie Book and Beanie Forum. I check all of the club's e-mail boxes and answer questions. I am the judge who reads all of the contest entries. I do a lot of typing! When I have the time, I like to find links to websites we can add to the page. I "continually" (his word) "occasionally" (my word) make suggestions to the Beanie Master about changing something around. He doesn't get out very much these days...

What are some of the things people can do on the club page?

Our goal for our club page is to make it as interactive as possible so kids and adults can write to each other, express opinions, ask questions, and find answers to their Beanie questions. We want it to be a fun place where people can meet new friends and talk about their favorite Beanies!

Every month we have a PrezQuiz. Heather asks a question about Beanie Babies and everyone can e-mail their answers. In the Voting Booth you can vote for your favorite Beanie Baby. You can talk to others in the BBB Club Chatter Box.

You can see what others have said in the Beanie Book then sign it yourself, or you can leave messages in the Beanie Forum and get replies from others. We proudly feature Beanie articles written by Ms. Janie Daniels, our club's Investigative Reporter. There are also many links to other Beanie webpages that will lead you to the "latest Beanie news."

I understand that you are a kindergarten teacher. Have you ever used Beanie Babies as a learning tool?

Yes, but I also use other brands of bean-filled toys as well. Beanies became scarce right after Christmas, 1996. I did not want to create even more disappointment for my students by promoting something I knew they couldn't get, so I downplayed owning a "TY" Beanie Babie. Instead, I encouraged owning and loving all kinds of bean bag toys in my classroom. Any bean bag critter was welcome in our room as long as it followed our rules and played well with others. Not surprisingly, all of our beanie visitors were always well-behaved. It was obvious many of the Beanies my students brought in were also very well-loved!

Which Beanie Babie is your favorite and why?

Radar is my favorite. He is the first Beanie I bought for myself. My twins had been collecting Beanie Babies since their birthday in May, 1996. It was early in November and I had just finished teaching one of my favorite units on "BATS" in my Kindergarten class. I took my nine year old twins Beanie hunting and found Radar in a nearby Hallmark store. I knew he was mine the minute I saw him! He will make an appearance in my classroom this October when "bats" will once again be the topic of discussion.

Please sum up the term "Beanie Babies" in twenty five words or less.

The next time I go Beanie hunting I hope I can find Tuffy!!

CHAPTER NINETEEN

Ms. Janie's Top Ten Beanie Favorites

1. Liberty
   Liberty reminds me of how patriotic I am and how much I love my country.
   The flag represents a symbol all Americans can be proud of.

2. Rex
   After trying for many months, Rex was my first Dinosaur trade. I wish Ty would create more Dinosaurs. Rex's tie-dyed coloring is fascinating.

3. Magic
   Magic allows me the opportunity to use my imagination and dream about what could have been. The wings on Magic can mesmerize and hold my attention while I dream.

4. Maple

Maple is the first Beanie Babie I purchased from another country.
Maple appears to me as though he wears his Canadian Flag showing a lot of pride.

5. Garcia

Garcia would qualify as one of my favorites because it's a Teddy Bear and I love Teddy Bears. It's color variation is nothing short of a stroke of genius.

6. Roary

I was born in the month of August. Roary reminds me of Leo the Lion, which resembles a strong and powerful figure.

7. Tuffy

I love small dogs and Tuffy is one of the cutest I've ever seen. I also was attracted to him because of his napped material and two tone color variation.

8. Inch

Not only are Inch's colors very bright and cheerful, they also remind me to slow down and enjoy life.

9. Jolly

I love Jolly's mustache and the way it's body bends.
In my opinion Ty naming this toy Jolly only indicates that they are trying to use names which make people feel good.

10. Valentino

Not only can this toy be used year around to display affection and love, it also presents a special kind of warm feeling when you hold it.

What Are Your Top Ten Favorites?

1.

2.

3.

4.

5.

6.

7.

8.

9.

10.

CHAPTER TWENTY

Kitty's Opinion

Featuring Kitty, Owner and operator of "Bears By The Sea"

Of the many individuals I've spoken with, I always found Kitty to be a safe reliable source and a great inspiration whose opinion I value.

I have purchased from Bears By The Sea on a few occasions and have always been pleased with their service. I also find their web site to be outstanding.

Please provide a bio on yourself.

B.A. degree in Education
A.S. degree in Nursing (Registered Nurse)
Own Pacific Leisure Marketing (Internet Marketing Business that has designed and maintains over 60 web sites all over the world. We also do digital brochures, catalogs, and digital photography. We also sell software, and computer components for system upgrades.)

Please tell us a little about your store (Bears By The Sea)

> Opened 1992
> Tourist location in Pismo Beach, CA
> Half way between LA and San Francisco
> Open every day except Christmas

What made you decide to carry Beanie Babies?

> Inexpensive plush item for children to purchase

How long have you been dealing with the Ty company and do you carry any other Ty products?

> I have carried the full TY line since I opened in 1992.

What is your opinion of the Ty company?

> They are experiencing problems in processing orders.

Do you find that shipments are starting to arrive on a regular basis now?

> No

In your opinion, why do you feel Ty has had so many production problems?

> Poor organization

How popular are Beanie Babies in California?

> Moderately popular—not insane

Which Beanie Babie is your favorite, and why?

Seaweed the otter.
We have otters here in Pismo Beach.

Your web site (Bears By The Sea) is outstanding. In my opinion your site contains a lot of knowledgeable information and also allows individuals to get involved by using your on-line forum. Please explain how many hours a day you dedicate to this site and what inspires you to operate it.

We have been online for over two years. We try to provide a lot of good information for collectors. Our goal is to have a site where collectors can come to gather accurate information and discuss their collections with other collectors.
Around 25 percent of our sales are from the Internet. We spend several hours a day maintaining our web sites.
We created the Teddy Bear Store Directory:
http://webmill.com/bears/dir
This directory lists Teddy Bear Stores all over the world. Collectors and store owners help us keep it one of the most up-to-date directories.
We also created the Teddy Bear Orphanage:
http://webmill.com/bears/orphans
A place where bears and other plush animals can be put up for adoption to loving homes.

Many individuals which I have spoken with feel that the Beanie popularity has faded to some degree. In your opinion, does their popularity still remain strong?

We have seen some of the secondary market prices dropping. Our online voting poll indicates that interest is decreasing.

Please sum up Beanie Babies in twenty five words or less.

Fun and frustrating at the same time.

CHAPTER TWENTY-ONE

Interview with Nancy—
the originator and creator of the world's most popular Beanie Tote Bags

Beanie accessories are easier to find than Beanies in most cases. I have purchased many accessories and have found a wide variety available.

One day while reading a very popular web site, (Magan's Beanie Babies), I found a posting for a woman who made Beanie Totes. I ordered the totes as gifts and anticipated their arrival.

When the totes arrived, I was delighted. The quality was superior and the script writing was one of the best I'd ever seen.

I shared the product with many of my friends and store owners. Many of them placed orders for their own totes.

Whenever there is a product created with the quality as this one, I feel compelled to share it with the world. I have ordered seven totes and plan to order more for Christmas.

Because Nancy is the original creator of these tote bags, and because she is such a delightful person, I feel she rightfully deserves a place in my book.

155

Bio:

Nancy McCaffrey, married, two children ages 9 and 11, works part time as a school bus driver for middle and elementary aged children, 44 yrs. old.

Which is your favorite Beanie, and why?

Has to be Garcia! He's so cute and colorful not to mention it reminds me of the 60's tie-dyed decade.

What prompted you to make the Beanie accessories?

My daughter had an unfortunate accident on a neighbor's trampoline and broke her arm, requiring immediate surgery that day to place pins in her arm to stabilize it. While she was recuperating, a good friend of mine presented her with her first two Beanies, Peanut and Goldie. Of course, all the while she was home recuperating from surgery, I was there with her. The better she felt, the more demanding she became and I finally devised a way to take a 'break' by telling her I was going into the sewing room to develop a tote bag for her new beanies. The rest is, as they say, history!!

Please give a brief description of your products.

There are two tote styles available for Beanie collectors, young and old. The original style, #1 is a portfolio style tote that opens flat to reveal six gussetted pockets on the inside to hold beanies. It is a denim outer fabric that can be personalized with a name, (e.g. Jessica's Beanies) and has cotton web handles and a snap closure.

The #2 style of tote is a box bottom blue jean tote with four outer pockets and can hold additional beanies inside, approximately 15. It also comes with personalized embroidery on the outside. It also has cotton webbed handles for ease of carrying.

(Discontinued as of 8-8-97: Teenie Beanie Tote which was a round bottom tote, with a webbed handle, and a fabric roll of ten pockets that tied like a sleeping bag when rolled up. It fits perfectly inside the tote when all 10 original McDonald Teenie Beanies were placed in the pockets. It was made of blue jean material and embroidered on the outside of the tote with "Teenie Beanie Tote.")

New products will be added mid-August, but not Beanie related. However, they will be in the tote line.

How successful have you been in selling your products?

It was incredible given that I had planned to sell a few, but quickly realized that incoming orders for two to three days for the first month was beyond my wildest expectations! A gentleman who runs the Meghan's Web Site about Beanies was kind enough to put my products on his web site and that's how I got started. After I discovered how much work he was doing for me, I decided to develop my own web site to relieve him of that time consuming task of updating it. The sales slowed considerably during the summer months, understandably, and picked back up as summer began to wane. I expect the holiday season will be strong again as Beanies are still a very hot item for both children and adults!

How many hours a day do you spend making, promoting, selling?

Depending on the number of orders outstanding, I usually confine my sewing to three days per week on average. It takes about an hour to make each tote from beginning to end, so the amount spent on them daily reflects the number of orders. I do try to pace myself so that I can still attend to work, children, house, etc. Sometimes the laundry just doesn't get done in a very timely manner—I often borrow the washer and dryer for my Beanie tote materials! The promotion of the product is strictly word of mouth from past customers and of course, the web site and links others have been so generous to place in their web sites for me. I have not been aggressive in the promotional end of the business because I am but one person and can only make so many totes per week at best. Both my husband and father have mentioned hiring others to help me—but then that takes the fun out of it, makes it too much like a business, and less personal for me!

Please sum up Ty Warner and Beanie Babies:

An incredible product, properly priced and certainly, I am sure, beyond even Ty Warner's expectations! People have compared this success to Cabbage Patch Dolls and Pet Rocks…oh, no, it's much bigger and of a longer duration than that, as it has broad appeal to all ages, therefore, guaranteeing its continued success for a long time to come!

Please provide the location where your products can be viewed for sale:

Currently the best place to see the totes is the following web address: http://www.beanietotes.com
Of course, you could view them from someone you may know who has purchased one in the past! You can also contact me via the web site if you need to see actual photos; I have been known to send a few of those out to people!

CHAPTER TWENTY-TWO

Beanie Games

Beanie Baby IQ Contest

About the contest:

You will be given a set of questions to answer, after each question you will also be given a clue. This clue will either help you decide which site you need to go to in order to find the answer, or will give you other details.

Rules for the Contest:

HAVE FUN!!!!!!

Questions are as follows:

1. Can you name the original nine Beanie Babies and which two were just retired?

    Clue—I'm found on most Beanie Baby sites and also on a lot of wish lists. Don't be fooled by dates!!

2. What popular web site sounds like a fruit?

    Clue—The color is yellow!!

3. What does BBBClub stand for?
   Clue—Read main page.

4. I make Beanie Babie Tote Bags and Teenie Beanie Bags.
   Who am I?
   Clue—Site can be found on the BBB Club main page.

5. Which Beanie Baby has a birthday that is June 15th?
   Clue—Dog.

6. Which Beanie Baby has a birthday that is July 15th?
   Clue—Bear

7. What am I and what is my name?
   Clue—Bipity Bopity Boo! I was turned into a horse on a
   favorite Disney kids' movie.

8. What were the names of the 10 Teenie Beanies sold in
   McDonalds Happy Meals?
   Clue—Check Teenie Beanies on Beanie Web sites.

9. What is Maple's Birthday and his poem?
   Clue—Maple's home site or BeanieMom.

10. In Kids' Survey—"Hey Kids What's Up With
    Ty"…What was the number 1 answer for the following
    question: "What do you think about Ty only allowing
    stores to order once a month and only 36 of each
    piece?"
    Clue—Check out the Kid's Survey in this book.

Answers can be found on the next page.

Nancy's World Famous Beanie tote Bag.

Answers

1. ANSWER—Legs, Squealer, Cubbie, Flash, Splash, Patti, Chocolate, Spot and Pinchers. Flash and Splash were just retired on May 11, 1997.

2. ANSWER—Our British Connection: Lemon Lainey Design, http://www.lemonlaineydesign.com

3. ANSWER—Beanie Babies Buddies Club http://www.netreach.net/~rjones/beanie.html

4. ANSWER—Nancy makes the tote bags. Her page is called From The Heart HomePage. htp://www.beanietotes.com

5. ANSWER—Scottie

6. ANSWER—Blackie

7. ANSWER—In Disney's animated movie "Cinderella," a mouse was turned into a horse. Two of the mice were named Gus and Jaq. The Beanie baby that is a mouse is named Trap.

8. ANSWER—Patti, Pinky, Chocolate, Chops, Goldie, Speedy, Seamore, Snort, Lizz and Quacks

9. ANSWER —Maple's birthday is July 1st, and his poem is:
Maple the bear likes to ski
With his friends, he plays hockey
He loves his pancakes and eats every crumb
Can you guess what country he's from?

10. ANSWER—It stinks!

Scramble

The following are the "scrambled" names of new Beanies released 1/1/97! How fast can you "unscramble" them???

1. EML _____

2. IPHPYTI _____

3. TSNU _____

4. PHIYTPO _____

5. PSIN _____

6. AERIGC _____

7. CHRNCU _____

8. COPHU _____

9. BEOID _____

10. ECLEFE _____

11. OTRSN _____

12. IPFTYPLO _____

13. RENBIE _____

Look at the bottom of the page for the ANSWERS...

Answers: 1. Mel 2. Hippity 3. Nuts 4. Hoppity 5. Snip 6. Gracie 7. Crunch 8. Pouch 9. Doby 10. Fleece 11. Snort 12. Floppity 13. Bernie

Word Search

Here is another word game for you to enjoy.

```
A N I P M W S R A E
S L B E Z C J S L Y
P F L I P D G T M A
O Q E Y T A K U V D
T F G A R S I N C H
H K S C G B D O L C
A Z I P C O N G O U
P A F S B N H N P O
P L B Y T E R I J P
Y T A N K S G R A F
```

See if you can find the following Beanie names.

Bones, Congo, Doby, Ears, Flip, Garcia, Happy, Inch, Legs, Mel, Nip, Nuts, Pouch, Ringo, Sly, Spot, Tank, Zip

Our Retired Beanie Friends Word Search

```
T W K B S P I D E R H Q J F
L U A J E R L U B Z X L T K
P Q S K S L I T H E R U S B
R B I K M P K C P E T D E J
Z N H G C R O W S T W A S L
G E T S I R N H E A R X I H
M O Z G A L Q R C B P B D U
X C H L T K P H Z T E L I M
F T R E X E I Y A R K W S P
Y B C F P L S W T H X T E H
P A R T L B L Y I D I Q P R
C T H Y E M A C S N A K E E
H S I F L U M R G Q L X B Y
Y T N O R B B T A B A S C O
```

Bronty, Bumble, Chilly, Chops, Caw, Coral, Kiwi, Lefty, Peking, Rex, Steg, Sting, Trap, Flutter, Liberty, Slither, Tabasco, Web, Tusk, Humphery, Righty

EXTRAS: These names will tell what some of the above animals are, see if you can find them as well.

Bee, Spider, Snake, Ray, Bull, Fish, Lamb, Bear

Beanie Game Ideas

1. Put different Beanies in a bag, have the children feel inside the bag without looking and try to figure out which one it is.

2. Ask children to come up with their own Beanie, draw it, name it, date it, and put a poem to it.

3. Copy a picture of a Beanie, cut it into a puzzle, and have the kids put it back together.

4. Use Jello to make Beanie animals with cookie cutters.

5. Buy sticker paper, let the kids draw up their own Beanie stickers, and color or paint them.

6. Use play-do to make a Beanie animal.

7. Draw a portion of a Beanie and see if the kids can guess which Beanie you have.

8. Ask kids to describe their favorite Beanie without naming it, and see if the other kids can identify it.

9. Put a lot of the Beanie animal names in a bag, have the kids select one and see if they can act out that animal, the other kids have to match the Beanie name with the animal.

Question Corner

1. I'm hot as you can see, show red and run from me.
2. In 1982 I was on Reagan's side for the presidency (Republican).
3. In 1982 I was on Carter's side for the presidency (Democratic).
4. I stand for the USA and I'm proud of it!
5. Crossing deserts is my job.
6. Water is high and I'm down deep, step on me and I'll burn your feet.
7. I was a meat eater in "Jurassic Park."
8. I'm endangered and have huge teeth.
9. I rhyme with butter.
10. Where I live you will shiver and freeze.
11. I'm black as night with beak and feet bright as day.
12. Sweaters are made from me.
13. My neck reached the top of trees.
14. Spikes grow down my back, I was a plant eater.
15. I swam all day under the sea eating kelp and small water bugs.
16. In the jungle I do live, up high in a tree tons of things are below me.
17. A hive is my home, and some say I'm a pest , but I don't sting unlike others of my kind.
18. "Squeak" "Squeak" "Squeak" I'm not a cat toy.
19. My house of thin sticky string shimmers in the light.
20. I am slimy and crawl but I have no feet.
21. You can find me at the zoo, but don't pity me because of my black eye, it's natural.

WHO ARE WE???

ANSWERS: 1. Tabasco 2. Righty 3. Lefty 4. Libearty 5. Humphrey 6. Sting 7. Rex 8. Tusk 9. Flutter 10. Chilly 11. Caw 12. Chops 13. Bronty 14. Steg 15. Coral 16. Kiwi 17. Bumble 18. Trap 19. Web 20. Slither 21. Peking

May 1997 Releases:

Newly designed Beanie scramble and question corner game.

Read all questions carefully in order to unscramble the answers. The questions will have an association with the New Released Beanie names.

1. I can soar high in the sky. Who am I?
   Clue—LDYAB
2. I can be related to something that falls in the winter, my look alike is a different color. Who am I?
   Clue—DLZIBZAR
3. My name rhymes with Nip. Who am I?
   Clue—ICPH
4. I can crawl on the beaches and snip at your toes, some people even eat me. Who am I?
   Clue—UCLDEA
5. I'm annoying in the early morning hours. Who am I?
   Clue—ELODOD
6. I was featured in a very popular kids' movie and I also have a look-alike. Who am I?
   Clue—OTDYT
7. Some say I'm very cute, I splash around and wet your suit. Who am I?
   Clue—EOCH
8. My friends say I'm happy and——, I also have a counterpart which has been retired. Who am I?
   Clue—LJLYO
9. I have been known to pull a sled or two. Who am I?
   Clue—ONOKNA
10. I have been redesigned with love and——in mind. Who am I?
    Clue—ECPAE

11. Some people say my face is a mess, the wrinkles in it can show signs of stress. Who am I? Clue—GSPLUY
12. I played the part of king in a popular kids' movie. Who am I?
    Clue—YORAR
13. I am very cute and brown and I'll bite at your heels if you turn around. Who am I? Clue—FYUTF
14. Look at the ocean, and what do you see? Watch out because I may roll over you. Who am I?
    Clue—VSWAE

BEANIE WISH LIST OCTOBER 1, 1997

CURRENT

___Baldy the eagle
___Batty the bat
___Bernie the St. Bernard
___Blackie the black bear
___Blizzard the snow tiger
___Bones the brown dog
___Bongo the monkey
___Bucky the beaver
___Chocolate the moose
___Chip the brown/black cat
___Congo the gorilla
___Claude the tie-dye crab
___Crunch the shark
___Cubbie the brown bear
___Curly the brown curly bear
___Daisy the black/white cow
___Derby the horse
___Doby the doberman
___Doodle the tie-dye rooster
___Dotty the dalmatian
___Ears the brown bunny
___Echo the dolphin
___Fleece the lamb
___Floppity the lilac bunny
___Freckles the leopard
___Goldie the goldfish
___Gracie the swan
___Gobbles the turkey
___Happy the hippo
___Hippity the mint bunny
___Hoppity the rose bunny
___Inch the worm
___Inky the octopus
___Jolly the walrus
___Lizzy the lizard
___Lucky the ladybug
___Magic the dragon
___Mel the koala
___Mystic the unicorn

CURRENT

___Nanook the husky
___Nip the gold cat
___Nuts the squirrel
___Patti the platypus
___Peace the tie-dye bear
___Peanut the elephant
___Pinchers the lobster
___Pinky the flamingo
___Pouch the kangaroo
___Pugsly the pug dog
___Quackers the duck
___Ringo the raccoon
___Roary the lion
___Rover the red dog
___Scoop the pelican
___Scottie the terrier
___Seaweed the otter
___Sly the fox
___Snip the siamese cat
___Snort the bull
___Snowball the snowman
___Spike the rhinoceros
___Spinner the spider
___Spooky the ghost
___Squealer the pig
___Stinky the skunk
___Stripes the gold tiger
___Teddy the 1997 holiday bear
___Tuffy the terrier
___Twigs the giraffe
___Valentino the bear
___Waddle the penguin
___Waves the whale
___Weenie the dachshund
___Wrinkles the bulldog
___Ziggy the zebra
___Zip the black cat

RETIRED BEANIES

___Alley the alligator
___Bessie the brown/white cow
___Bronty the brontosaurus
___Bubbles the black/gold fish
___Bumble the bee
___Caw the crow
___Chilly the polar bear
___Chops the lamb
___Coral the tie-dye fish
___Digger the crab
___Flash the dolphin
___Flutter the butterfly
___Flip the white cat
___Garcia the tie-dye bear
___Grunt the razorback
___Hoot the owl
___Humphrey the camel
___Kiwi the toucan
___Legs the frog
___Lefty the donkey
___Libearty the bear
___Manny the manatee
___Peking the panda
___Radar the bat
___Rex the tyrannosaurus
___Righty the elephant
___Seamore the seal
___Slither the snake
___Sparky the dalmatian
___Speedy the turtle
___Splash the whale
___Spot the dog
___Steg the stegosaurus
___Sting the ray
___Tabasco the bull
___Tank the armadillo
___Teddy the brown bear
___Teddy the cranberry bear
___Teddy the jade bear
___Teddy the magenta bear
___Teddy the teal bear
___Teddy the violet bear
___Trap the mouse
___Tusk the walrus
___Velvet the panther
___Web the spider

I would like to thank the following people for contributing to this book.

Mike, Jennifer & David Daniels—My family

Randy & Sandy Jones—Owner of the Beanie Babies
    Buddies Club –
    http://www.netreach.net/~rjones/beanie.html

Magans Web site—Formally known as Magan's Beanie
    Babies – Now known as: BB World News and
    Information – http://www.geocities.com/Enchanted
    Forest/30981

Kevin & Elaine Smith—Lemon Lainey Web Site –
    http://www.lemonlaineydesign.com/

Kitty—Bears By The Sea –
    http://callamer.com/bears/tyguide.htm

Duncan—My Friend from England

Wendy—RJW's Web site – http://www.beaniemania.com/

Sara Nelson—Beanie Mom – http://www.beaniemom.com/

Les & Sue Fox—Authors of the book—*The Beanie Baby
    Handbook*

Susan & Ashley Melnichak—Best Friend and daughter

Nancy McCaffery—Beanie Totes
    –http://www.beanietotes.com/

Carolin Markiewich—Tin Can Alley

Bob Martin, Judy & Mary—Elmtree Stores

Wanda Blevins—McDonalds Supervisor

Linda & Tarnia Lara—Sister-In-Law and Niece

Sarah Collins—Friend

Beau Yarbrough—Reporter for the *Potomac News*

The Potomac News

Genny Ax—Editor

All of the stores and individuals who allowed me to interview them.